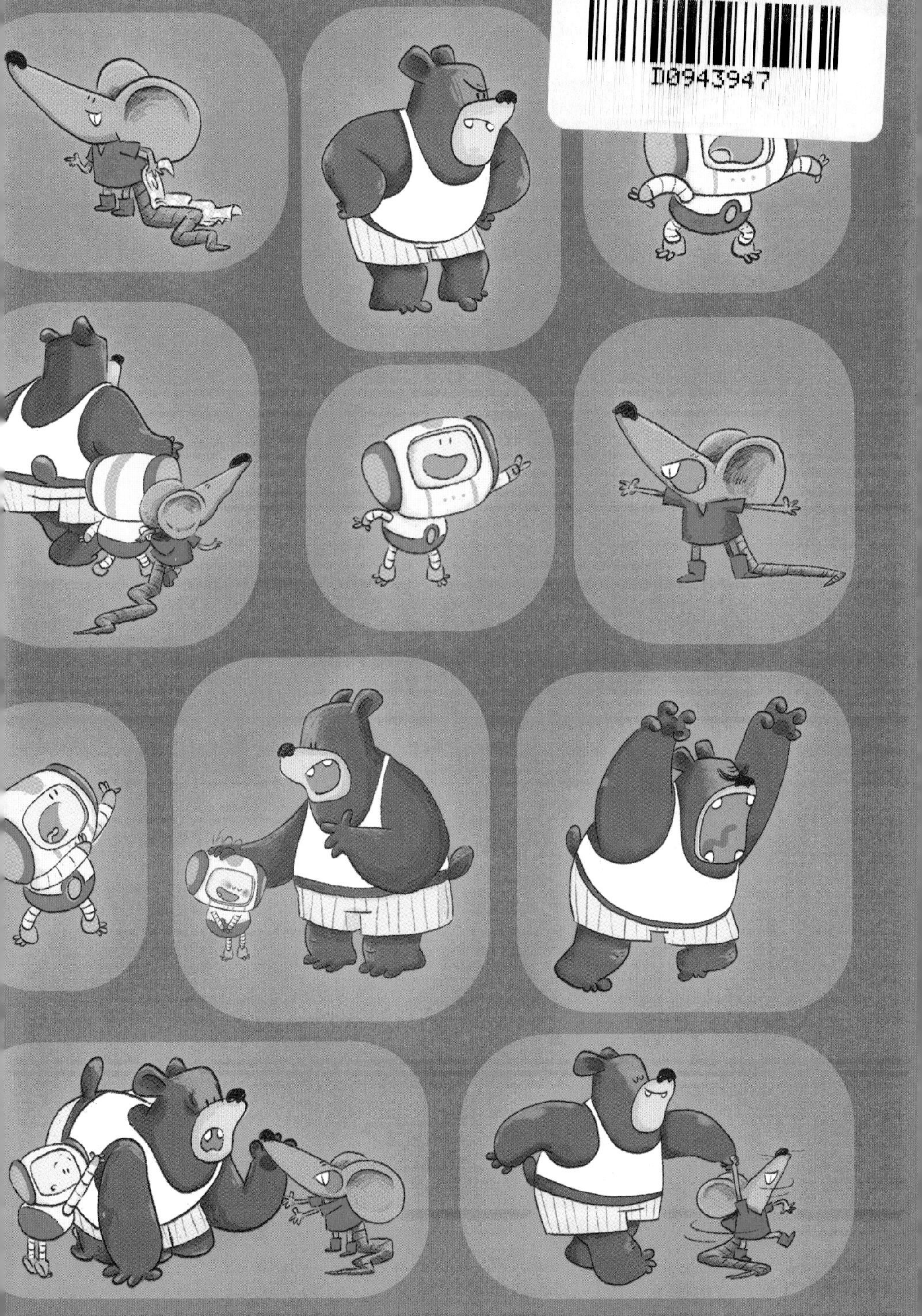

THE FOREST ROBOT

COPYRIGHT © 2022 BY SCHIFFER PUBLISHING, LTD.

ORIGINAL TITLE: BITMAX & CO.: *EL ROBOT DEL BOSQUE*
TEXT COPYRIGHT © 2020 JAUME COPONS
ILLUSTRATIONS COPYRIGHT © 2020 LILIANA FORTUNY
TRANSLATED FROM THE SPANISH BY SIMULINGUA, INC.
ORIGINALLY PUBLISHED IN CATALAN AND SPANISH BY COMBEL EDITORIAL,
AN IMPRINT OF EDITORIAL CASALS, SA

LIBRARY OF CONGRESS CONTROL NUMBER: 2021942725

ALL RIGHTS RESERVED. NO PART OF THIS WORK MAY BE REPRODUCED OR USED IN ANY FORM
OR BY ANY MEANS–GRAPHIC, ELECTRONIC, OR MECHANICAL, INCLUDING PHOTOCOPYING
OR INFORMATION STORAGE AND RETRIEVAL SYSTEMS–WITHOUT WRITTEN PERMISSION
FROM THE PUBLISHER.

THE SCANNING, UPLOADING, AND DISTRIBUTION OF THIS BOOK OR ANY PART THEREOF
VIA THE INTERNET OR ANY OTHER MEANS WITHOUT THE PERMISSION OF THE PUBLISHER IS
ILLEGAL AND PUNISHABLE BY LAW. PLEASE PURCHASE ONLY AUTHORIZED EDITIONS AND DO
NOT PARTICIPATE IN OR ENCOURAGE THE ELECTRONIC PIRACY OF COPYRIGHTED MATERIALS.

"SCHIFFER KIDS" LOGO IS A TRADEMARK OF SCHIFFER PUBLISHING, LTD.
AMELIA LOGO IS A TRADEMARK OF SCHIFFER PUBLISHING, LTD.

TYPE SET IN EGGWHITE/AVENIR NEXT ROUNDED

ISBN: 978-0-7643-6305-4
PRINTED IN INDIA

PUBLISHED BY SCHIFFER KIDS
AN IMPRINT OF SCHIFFER PUBLISHING, LTD.
4880 LOWER VALLEY ROAD
ATGLEN, PA 19310
PHONE: (610) 593-1777; FAX: (610) 593-2002
EMAIL: INFO@SCHIFFERBOOKS.COM
WEB: WWW.SCHIFFERBOOKS.COM

FOR OUR COMPLETE SELECTION OF FINE BOOKS ON THIS AND RELATED SUBJECTS,
PLEASE VISIT OUR WEBSITE AT WWW.SCHIFFERBOOKS.COM. YOU MAY ALSO WRITE FOR A
FREE CATALOG.

SCHIFFER PUBLISHING'S TITLES ARE AVAILABLE AT SPECIAL DISCOUNTS FOR BULK PURCHASES
FOR SALES PROMOTIONS OR PREMIUMS. SPECIAL EDITIONS, INCLUDING PERSONALIZED
COVERS, CORPORATE IMPRINTS, AND EXCERPTS, CAN BE CREATED IN LARGE QUANTITIES
FOR SPECIAL NEEDS. FOR MORE INFORMATION, CONTACT THE PUBLISHER.

MIX
Paper from
responsible sources
FSC
www.fsc.org   FSC® C016779

ons, Jaume, 1966-
max & Co. 1, The forest
ot /
22]
05254632114
06/14/23

THE
FOREST
ROBOT

COPONS & FORTUNY

Schiffer **Kids**™

4880 Lower Valley Road, Atglen, PA 19310

PART ONE

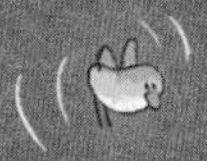

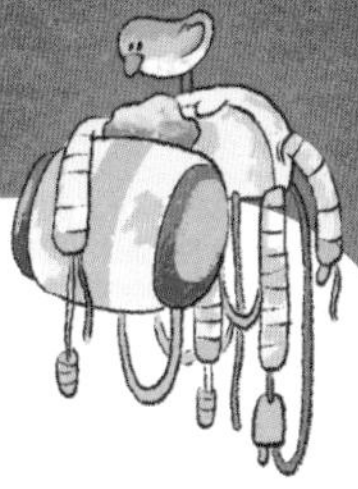

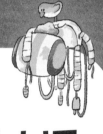

THE BLUE FOREST

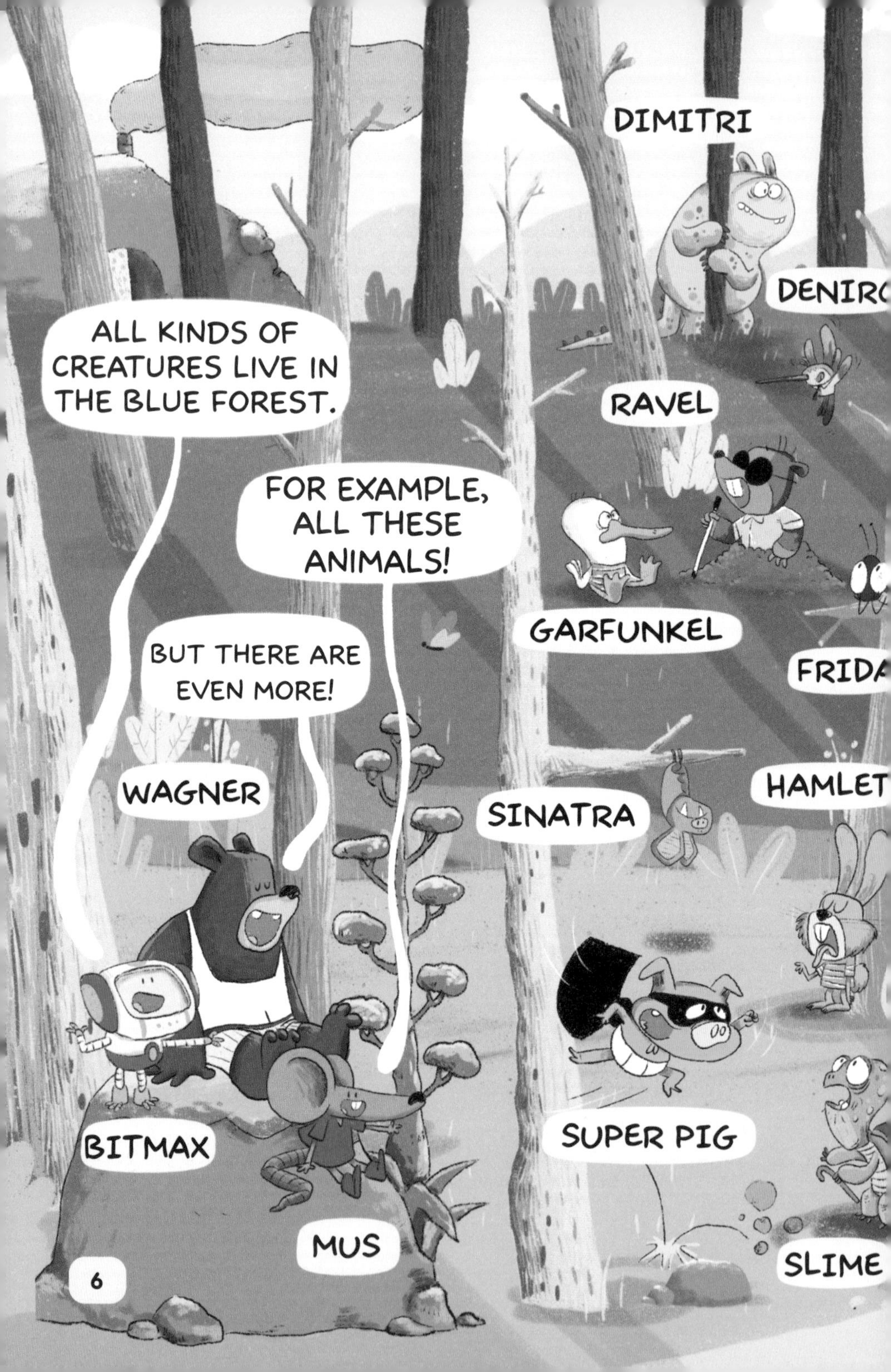
ALL KINDS OF CREATURES LIVE IN THE BLUE FOREST.
FOR EXAMPLE, ALL THESE ANIMALS!
BUT THERE ARE EVEN MORE!
DIMITRI
DENIRO
RAVEL
GARFUNKEL
FRIDA
WAGNER
SINATRA
HAMLET
BITMAX
SUPER PIG
MUS
SLIME

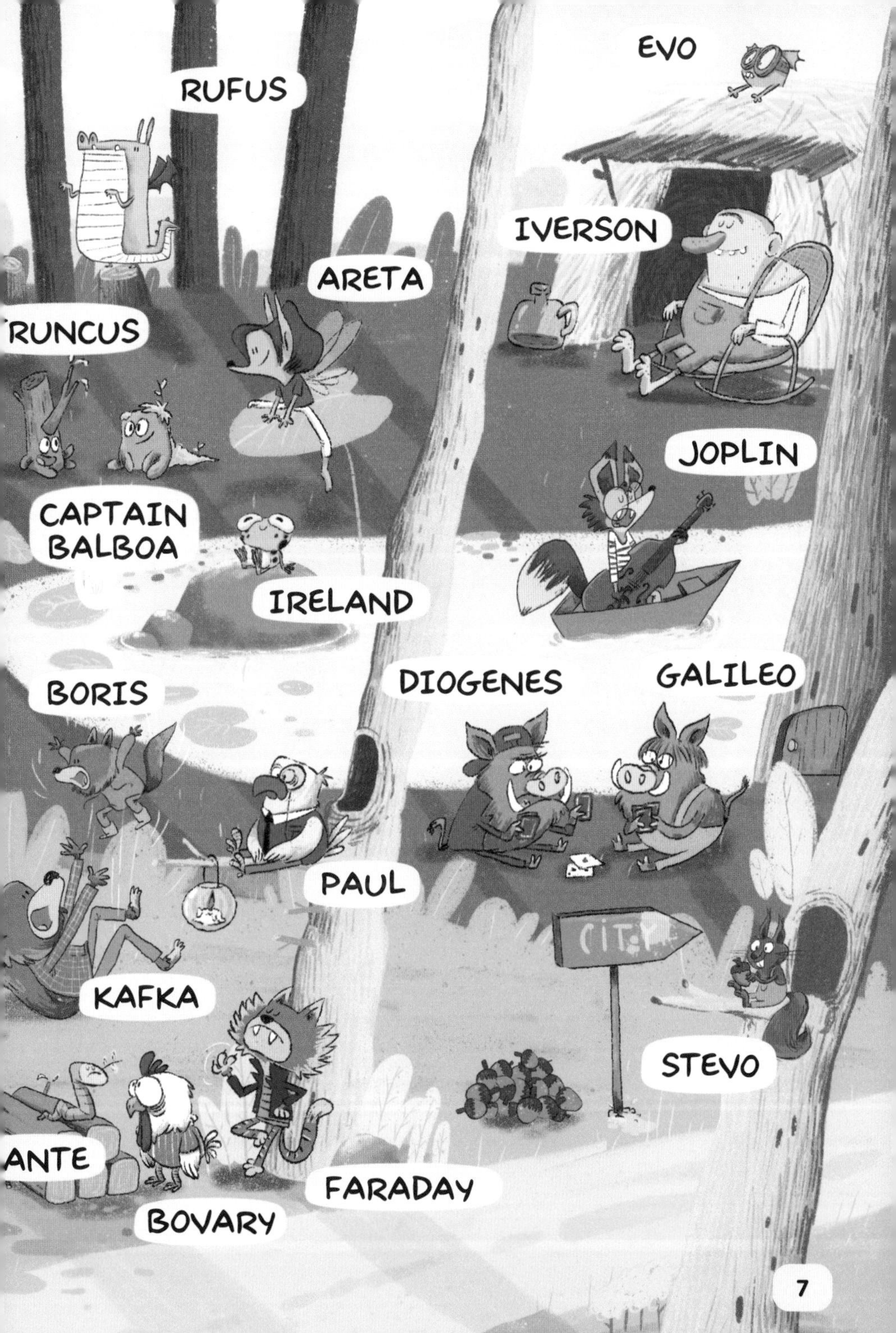
EVO
RUFUS
IVERSON
ARETA
TRUNCUS
JOPLIN
CAPTAIN BALBOA
IRELAND
BORIS
DIOGENES
GALILEO
PAUL
CITY
KAFKA
STEVO
ANTE
FARADAY
BOVARY

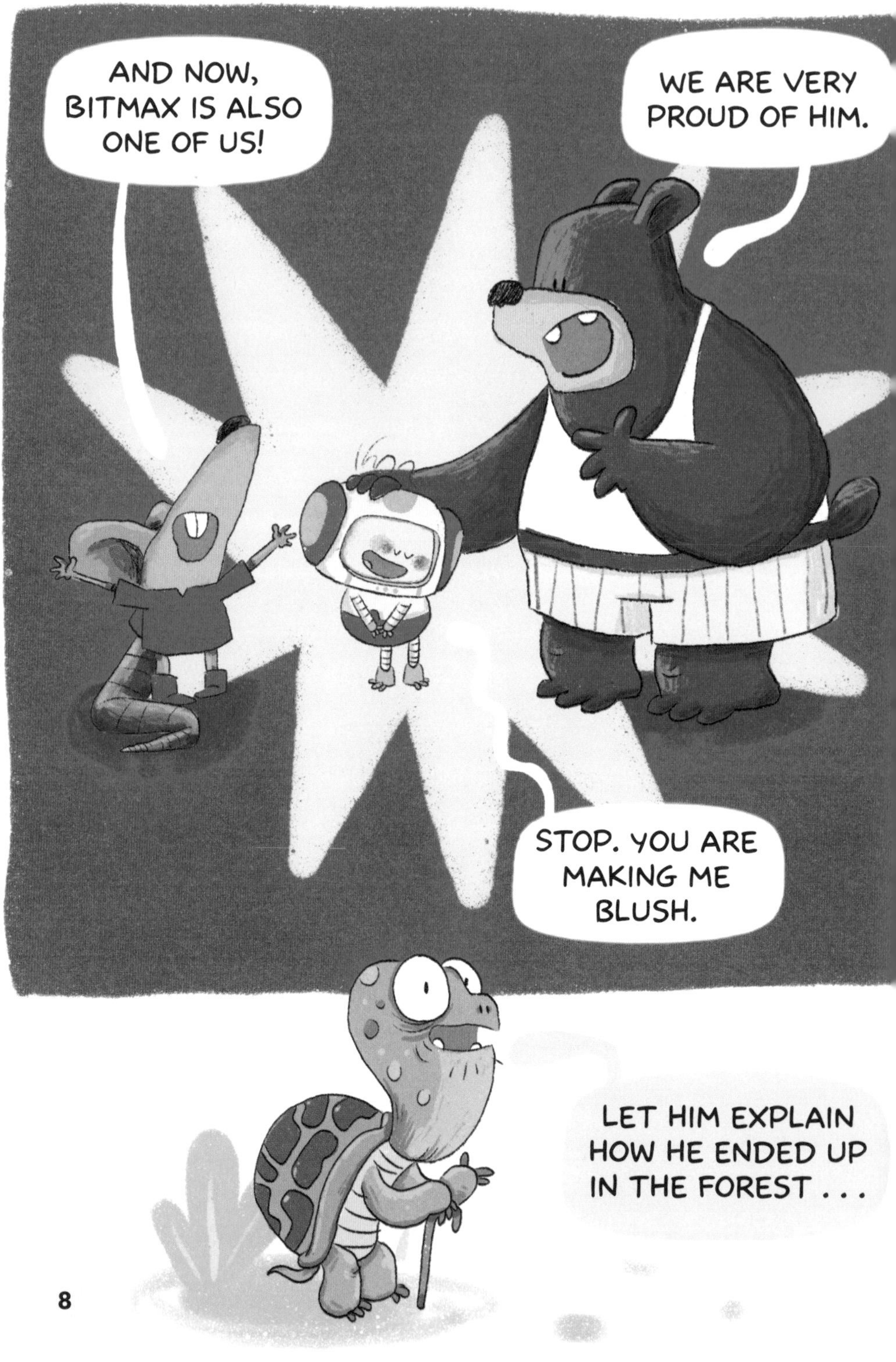
AND NOW, BITMAX IS ALSO ONE OF US!
WE ARE VERY PROUD OF HIM.
STOP. YOU ARE MAKING ME BLUSH.
LET HIM EXPLAIN HOW HE ENDED UP IN THE FOREST . . .

IT ALL STARTED BY THE ROCK ON THE ROAD, MUS AND WAGNER'S FAVORITE PLACE.

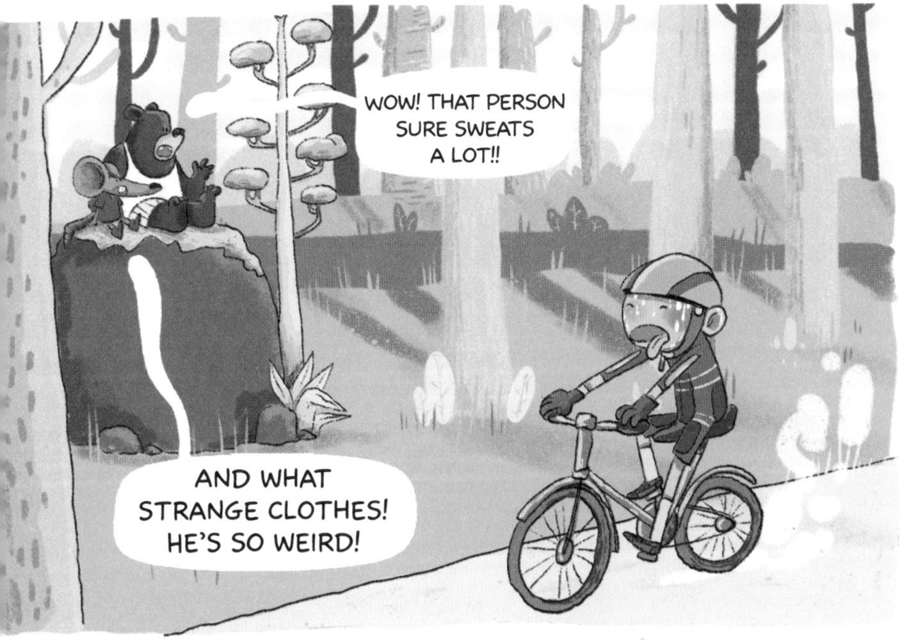
WOW! THAT PERSON SURE SWEATS A LOT!!
AND WHAT STRANGE CLOTHES! HE'S SO WEIRD!

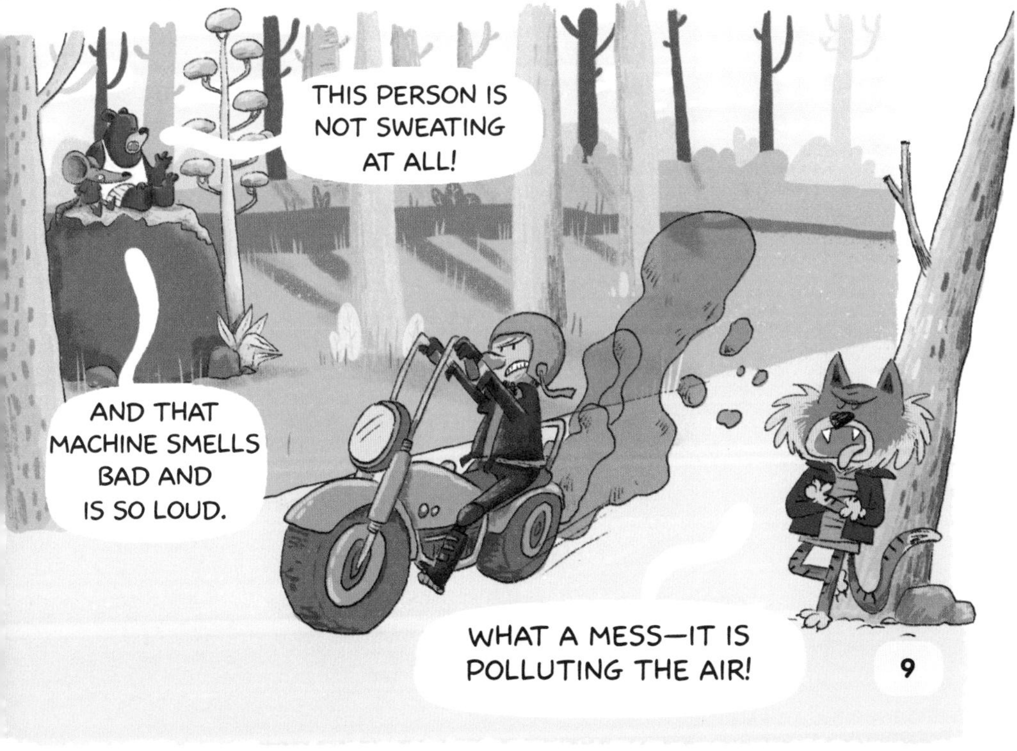
THIS PERSON IS NOT SWEATING AT ALL!
AND THAT MACHINE SMELLS BAD AND IS SO LOUD.
WHAT A MESS—IT IS POLLUTING THE AIR!

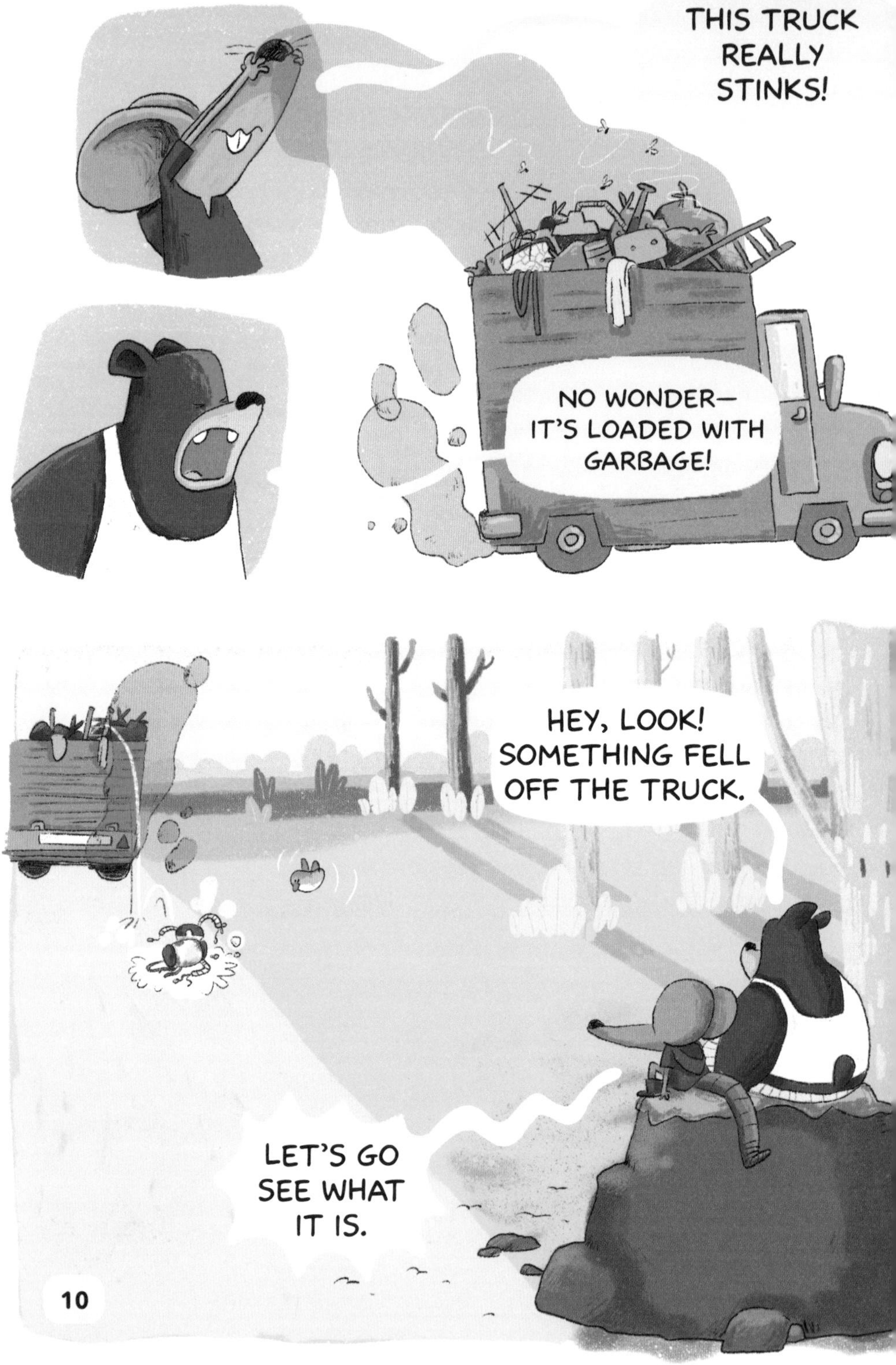
THIS TRUCK REALLY STINKS!
NO WONDER— IT'S LOADED WITH GARBAGE!
HEY, LOOK! SOMETHING FELL OFF THE TRUCK.
LET'S GO SEE WHAT IT IS.

WHAT IS THIS,
MUS?

CAN'T YOU SEE,
WAGNER? IT'S A
HOME ROBOT!

HOW DO YOU
KNOW THAT?

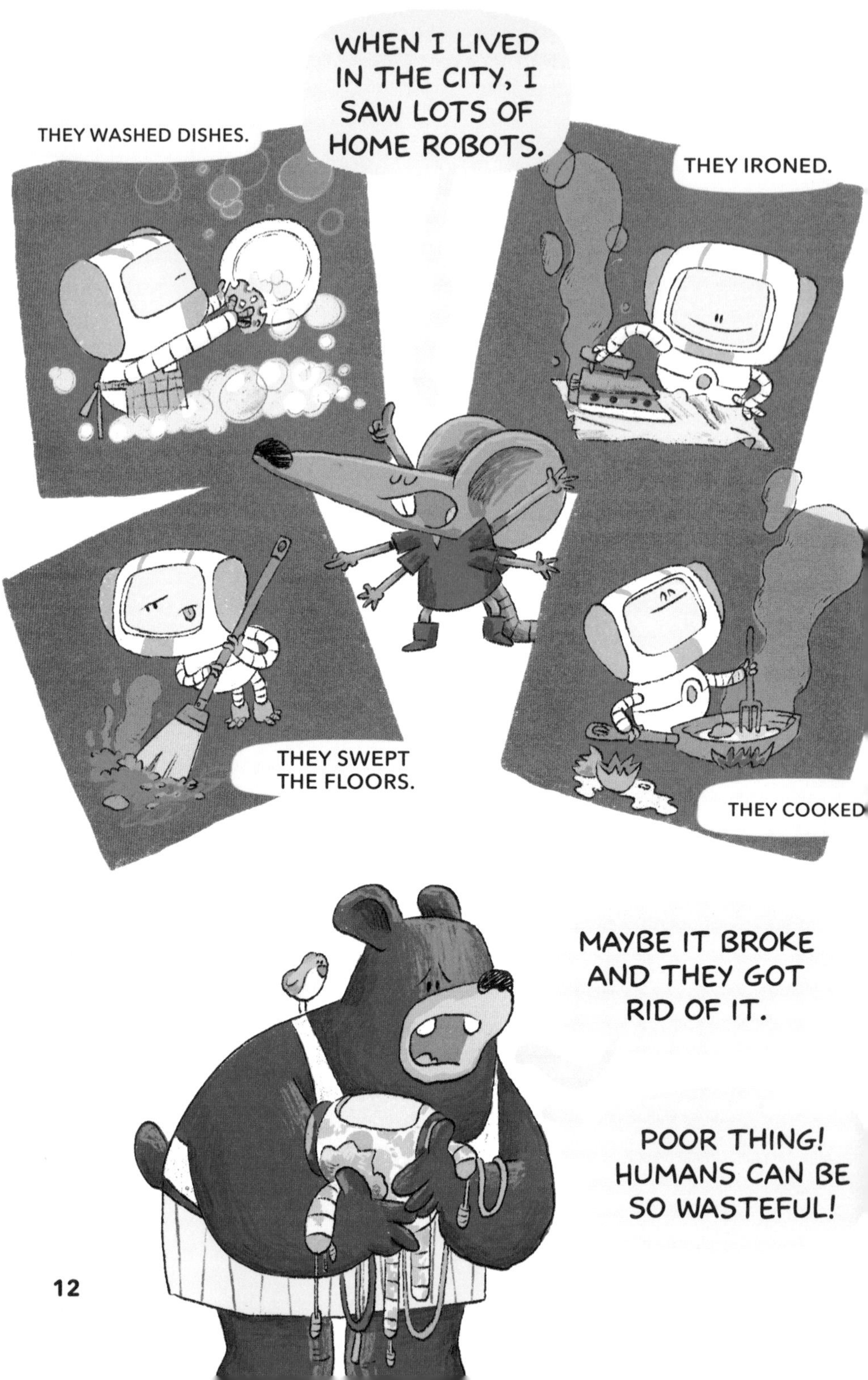
WHEN I LIVED IN THE CITY, I SAW LOTS OF HOME ROBOTS.
THEY WASHED DISHES.
THEY IRONED.
THEY SWEPT THE FLOORS.
THEY COOKED
MAYBE IT BROKE AND THEY GOT RID OF IT.
POOR THING! HUMANS CAN BE SO WASTEFUL!

AND THEN MUS AND WAGNER MADE A DECISION.

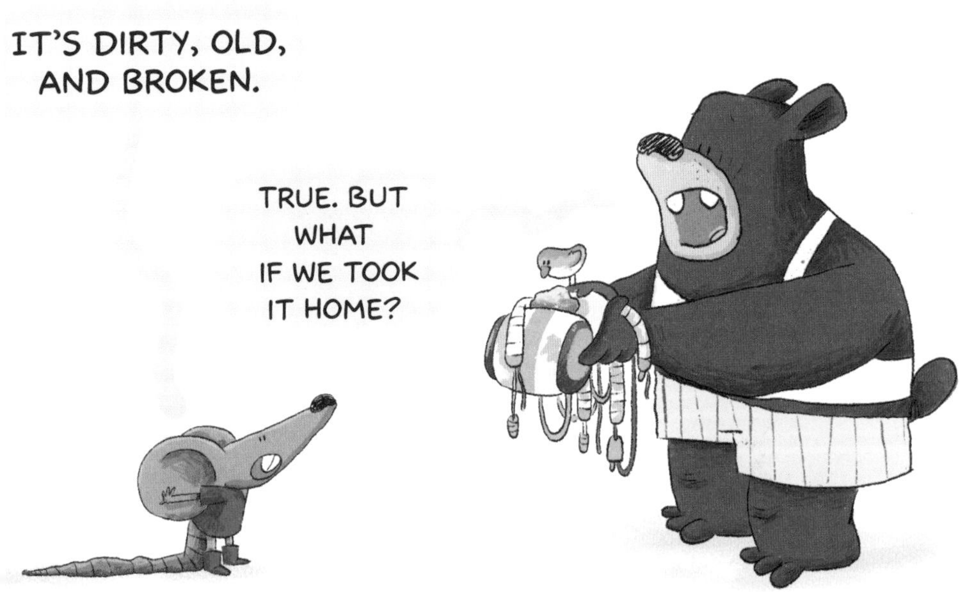
IT'S DIRTY, OLD, AND BROKEN.
TRUE. BUT WHAT IF WE TOOK IT HOME?

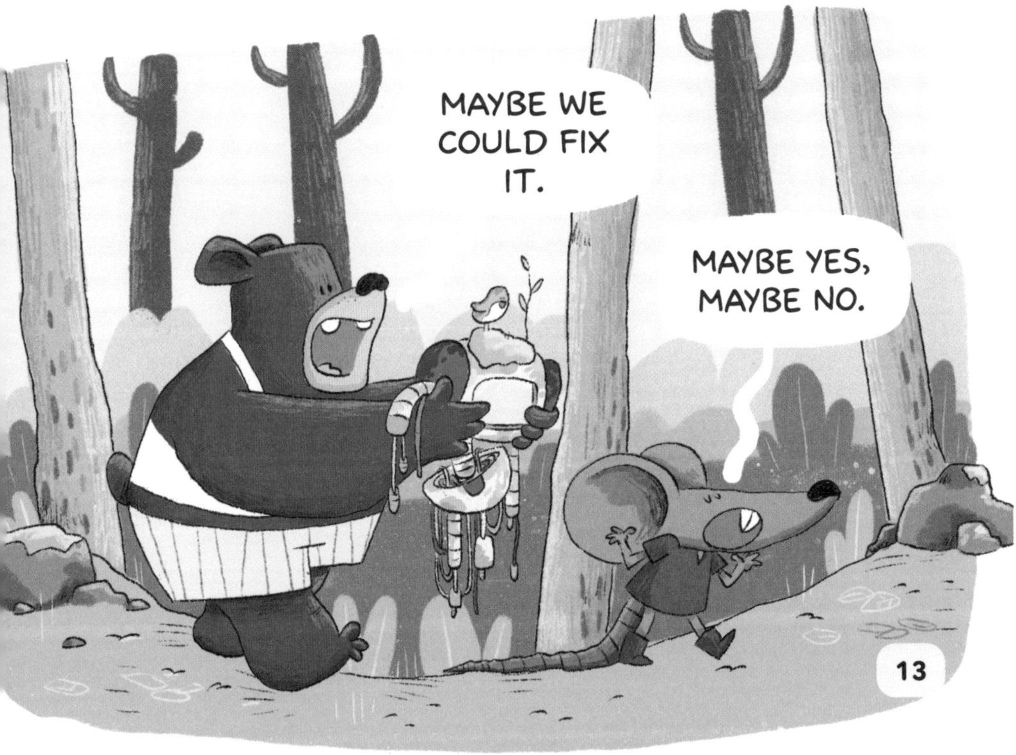
MAYBE WE COULD FIX IT.
MAYBE YES, MAYBE NO.

ONCE THEY TOOK ME HOME, THEY WASHED ME TOP TO BOTTOM AND TRIED TO GET ME TO START.

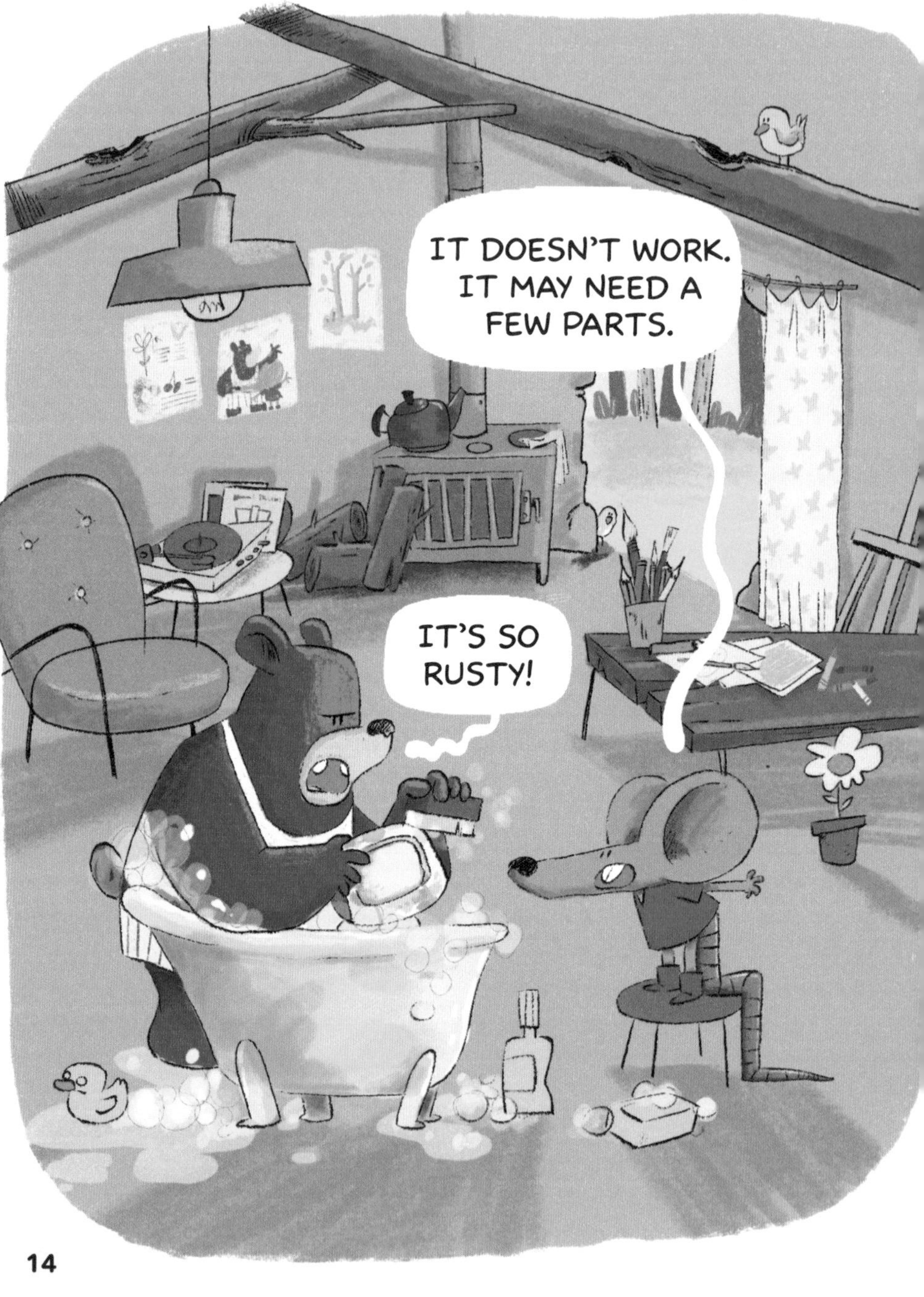
IT DOESN'T WORK. IT MAY NEED A FEW PARTS.
IT'S SO RUSTY!

MUS AND WAGNER FIXED ALL MY BROKEN PARTS.
THEY SPENT ALL NIGHT WORKING ON THE REPAIRS.

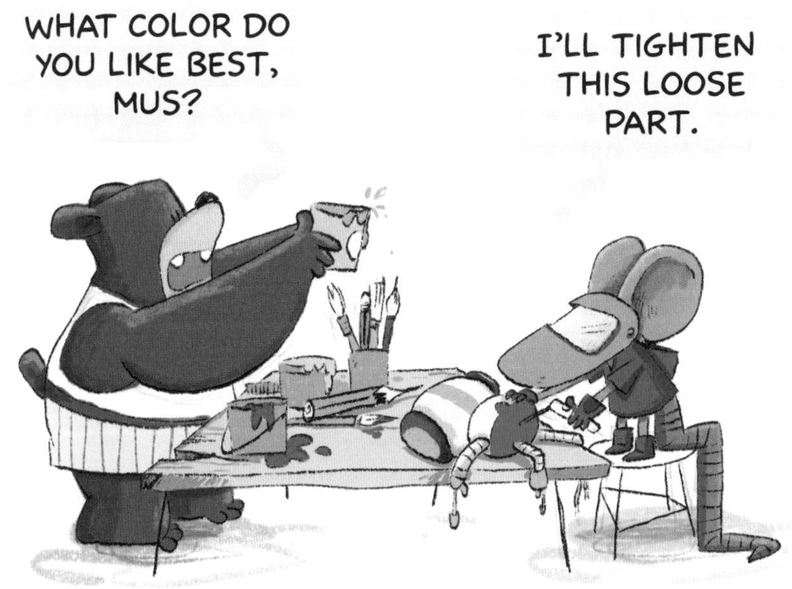
WHAT COLOR DO YOU LIKE BEST, MUS?
I'LL TIGHTEN THIS LOOSE PART.

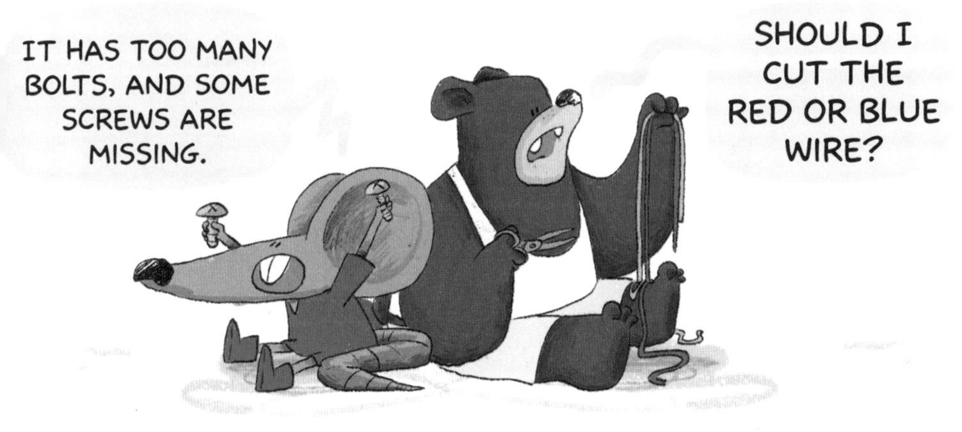
IT HAS TOO MANY BOLTS, AND SOME SCREWS ARE MISSING.
SHOULD I CUT THE RED OR BLUE WIRE?

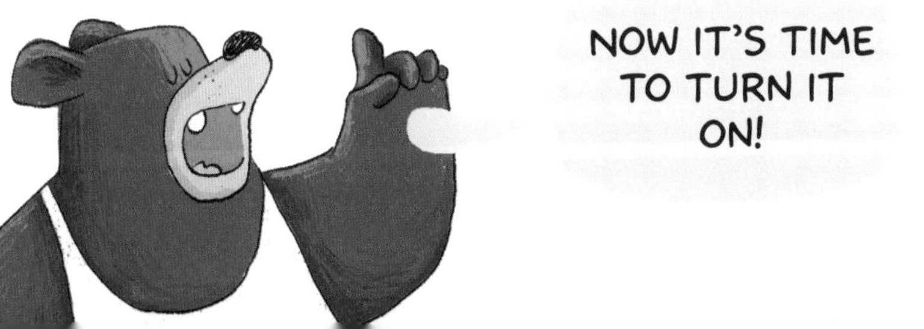
NOW IT'S TIME TO TURN IT ON!

AND THEN SUDDENLY . . .

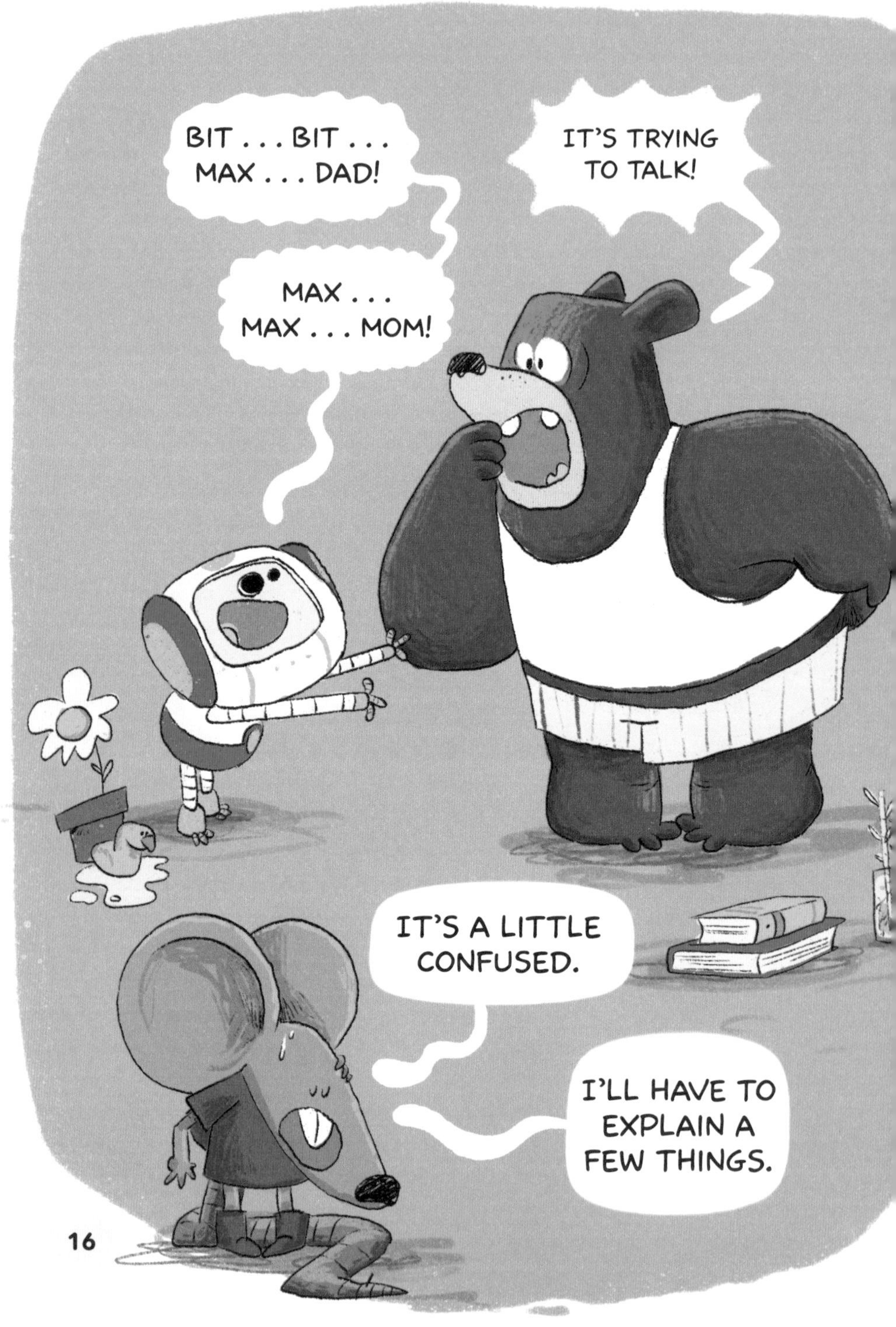
BIT . . . BIT . . .
MAX . . . DAD!
IT'S TRYING
TO TALK!
MAX . . .
MAX . . . MOM!
IT'S A LITTLE
CONFUSED.
I'LL HAVE TO
EXPLAIN A
FEW THINGS.

THE FOUR THINGS THAT MUS EXPLAINED TO ME:

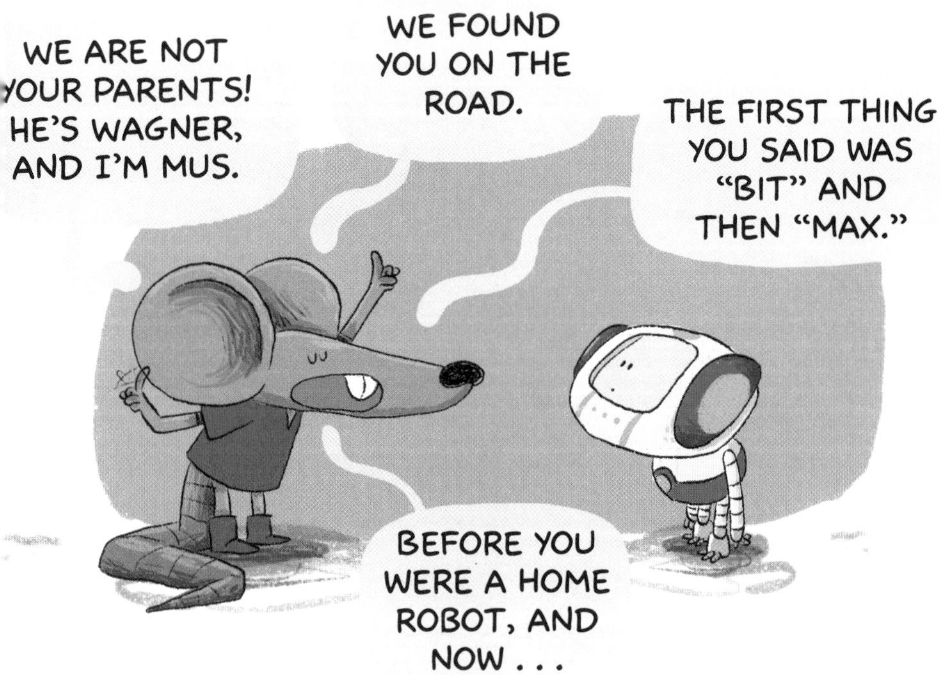
WE ARE NOT YOUR PARENTS! HE'S WAGNER, AND I'M MUS.
WE FOUND YOU ON THE ROAD.
THE FIRST THING YOU SAID WAS "BIT" AND THEN "MAX."
BEFORE YOU WERE A HOME ROBOT, AND NOW . . .

AND THIS IS WHAT I REPLIED:

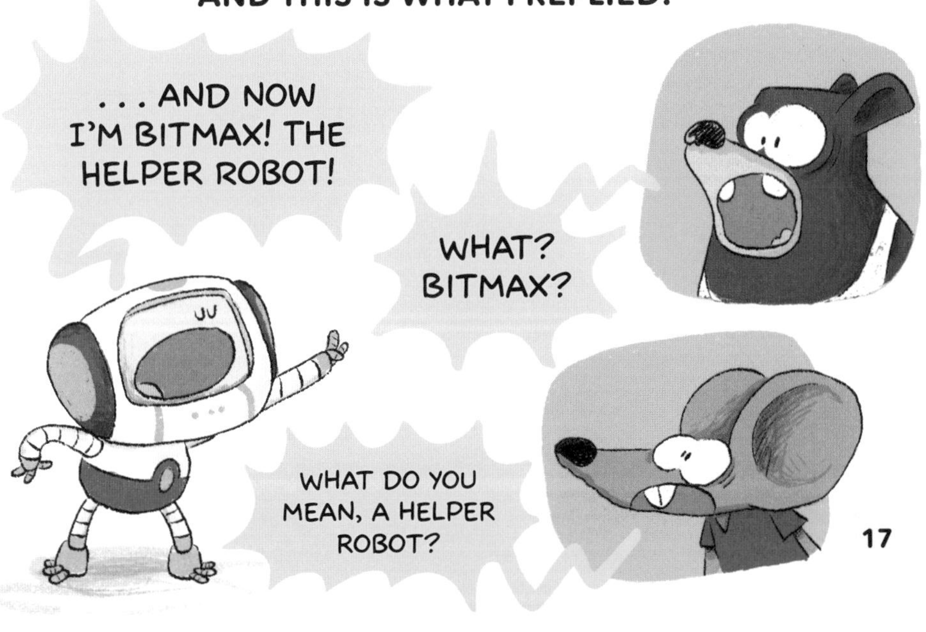
. . . AND NOW I'M BITMAX! THE HELPER ROBOT!
WHAT? BITMAX?
WHAT DO YOU MEAN, A HELPER ROBOT?

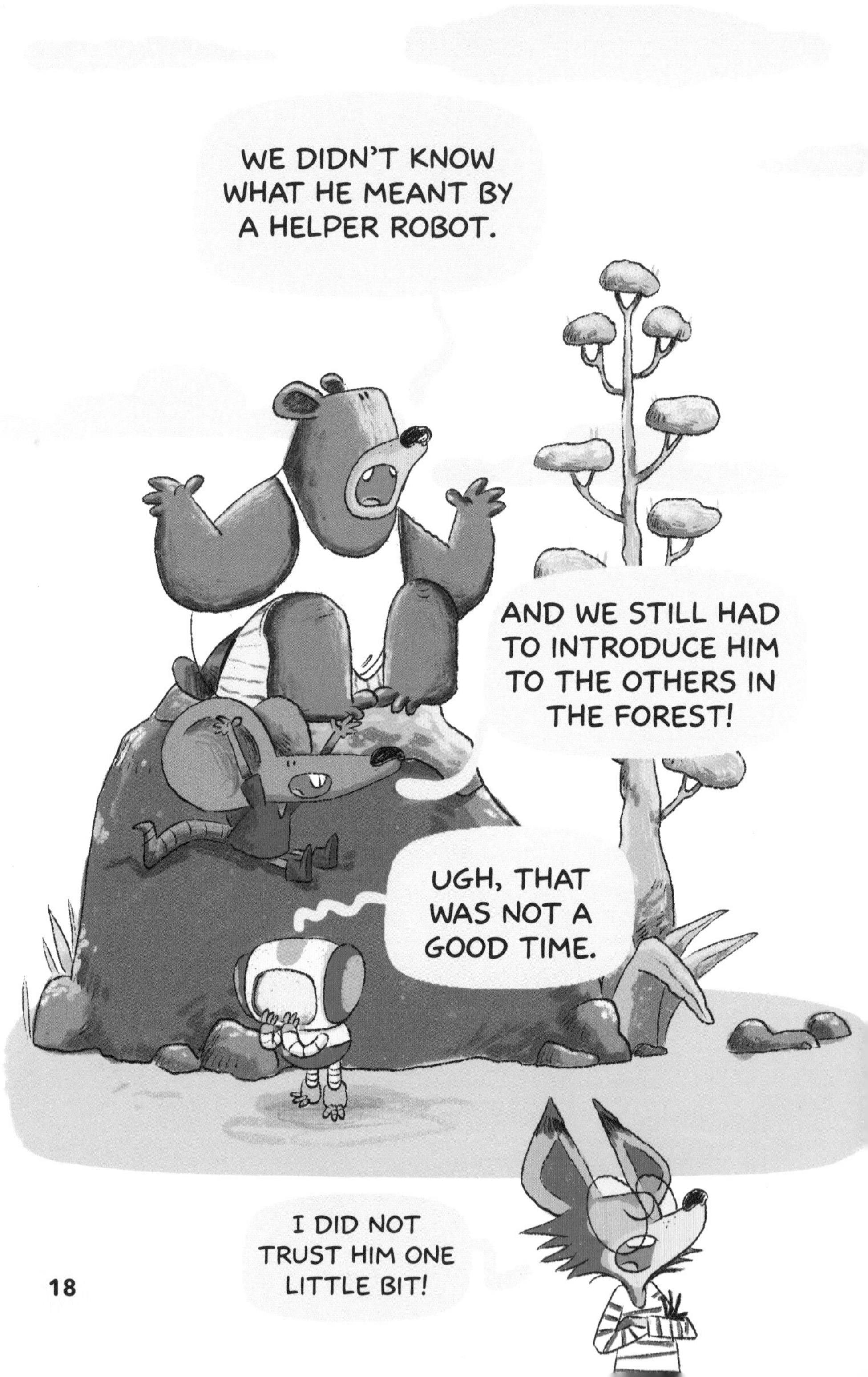
WE DIDN'T KNOW WHAT HE MEANT BY A HELPER ROBOT.
AND WE STILL HAD TO INTRODUCE HIM TO THE OTHERS IN THE FOREST!
UGH, THAT WAS NOT A GOOD TIME.
I DID NOT TRUST HIM ONE LITTLE BIT!

PART TWO

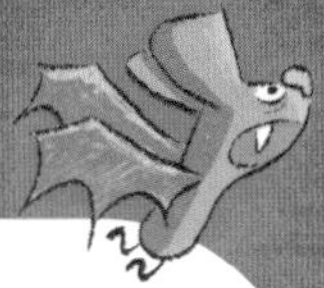

A ROBOT IN THE FOREST

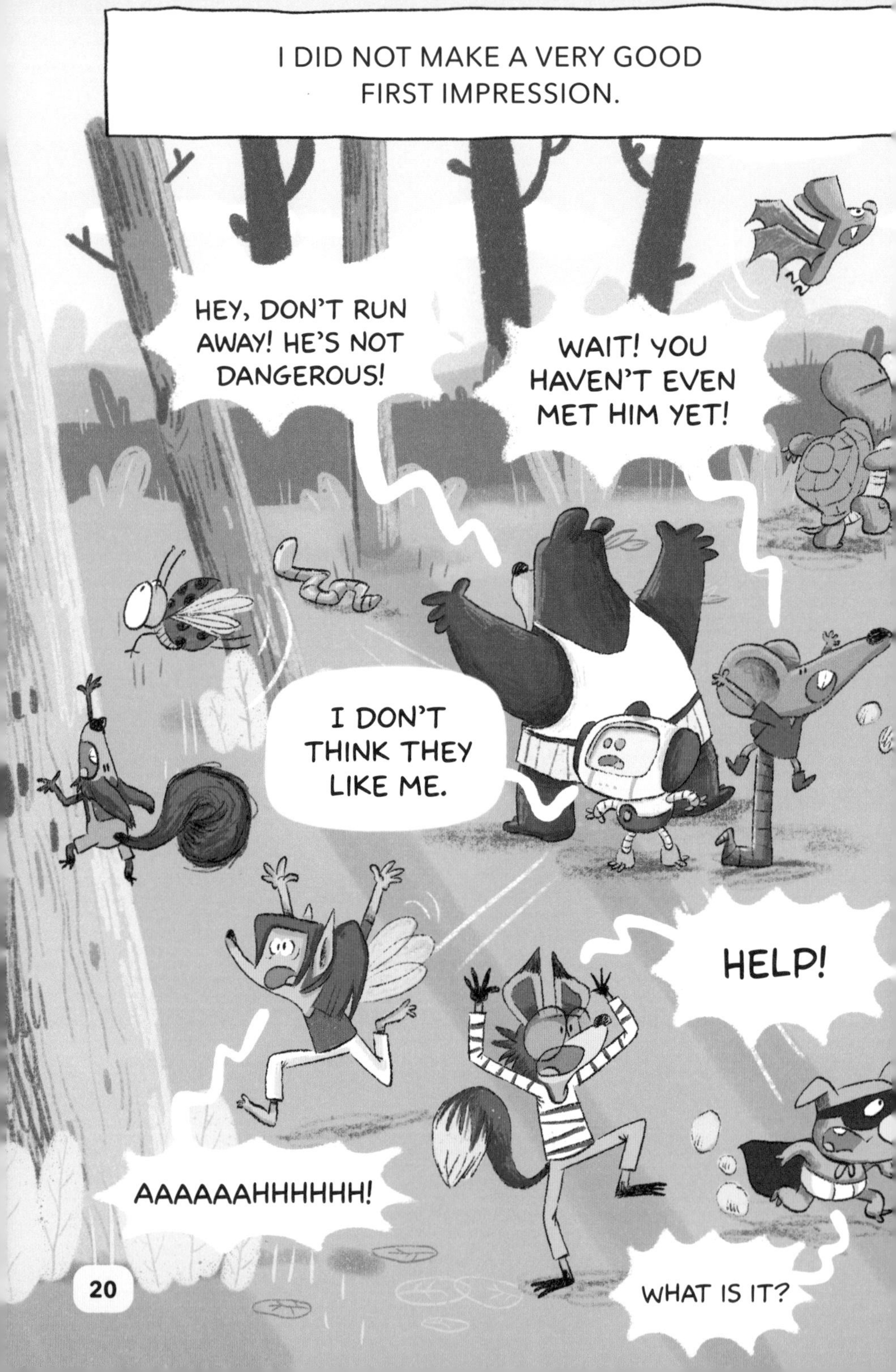
I DID NOT MAKE A VERY GOOD FIRST IMPRESSION.
HEY, DON'T RUN AWAY! HE'S NOT DANGEROUS!
WAIT! YOU HAVEN'T EVEN MET HIM YET!
I DON'T THINK THEY LIKE ME.
HELP!
AAAAAAHHHHHH!
WHAT IS IT?

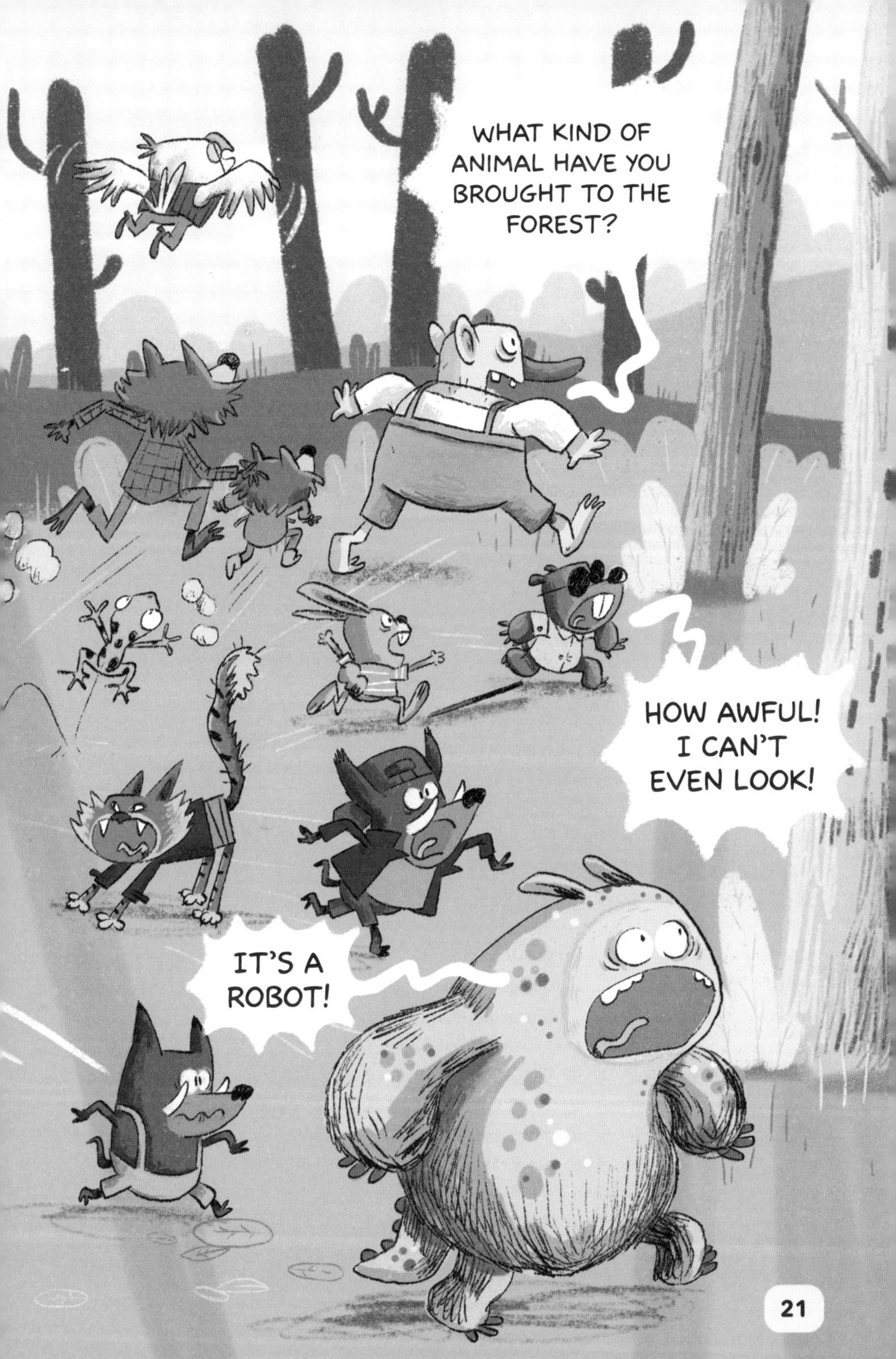
WHAT KIND OF ANIMAL HAVE YOU BROUGHT TO THE FOREST?
HOW AWFUL! I CAN'T EVEN LOOK!
IT'S A ROBOT!

NOBODY WAS SURE IF I SHOULD LIVE IN THE FOREST.

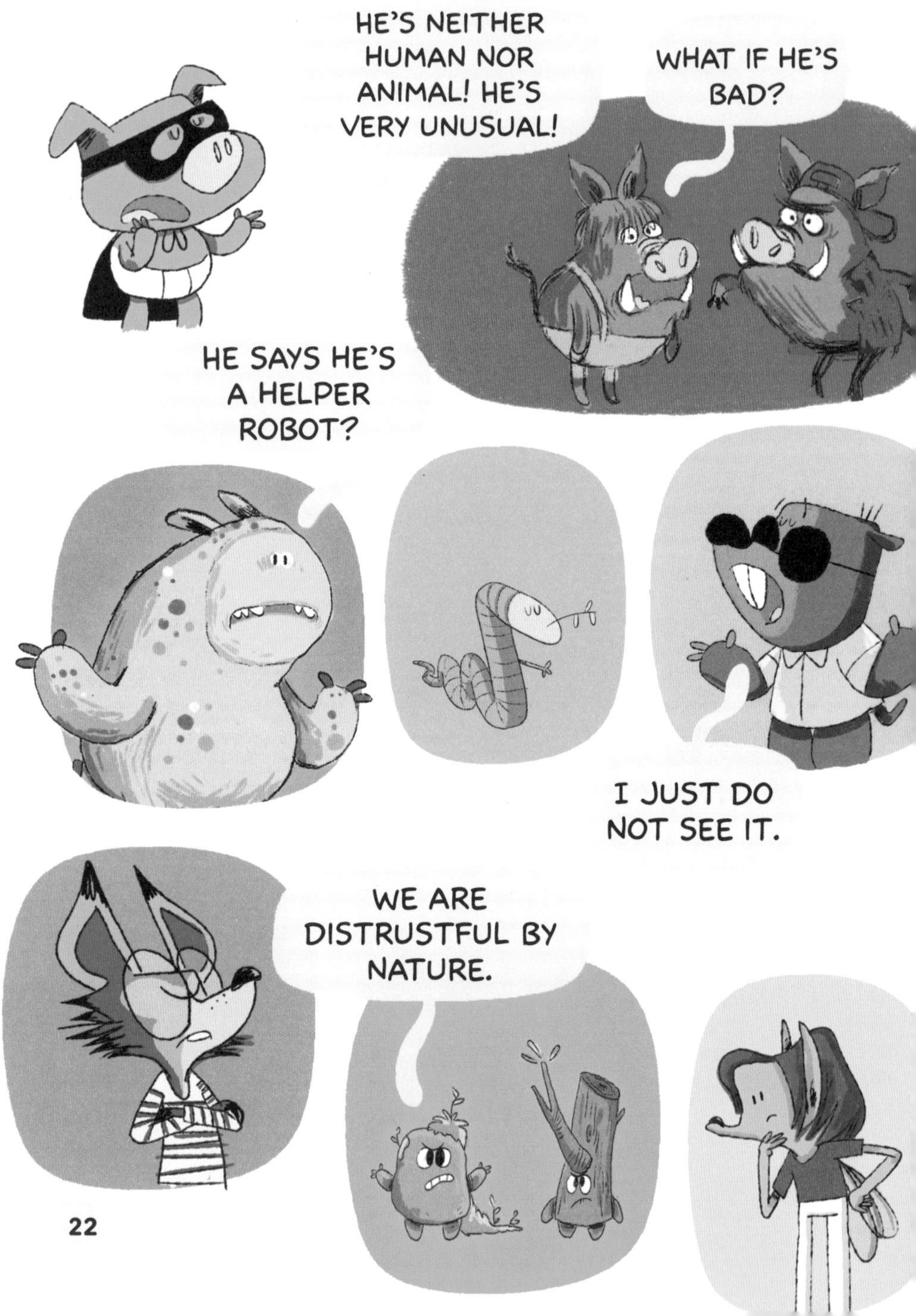
HE'S NEITHER HUMAN NOR ANIMAL! HE'S VERY UNUSUAL!
WHAT IF HE'S BAD?
HE SAYS HE'S A HELPER ROBOT?
I JUST DO NOT SEE IT.
WE ARE DISTRUSTFUL BY NATURE.

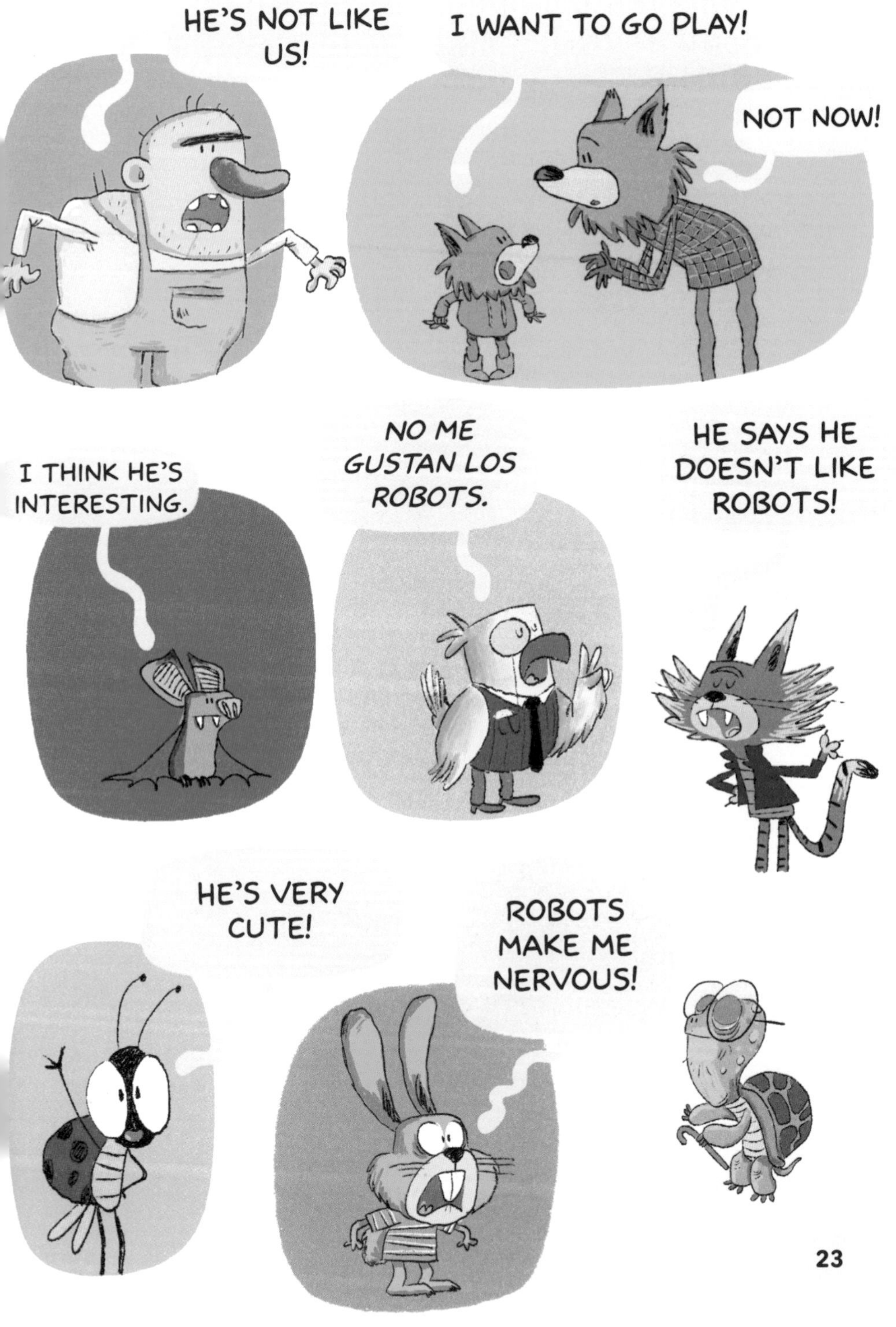
HE'S NOT LIKE US!
I WANT TO GO PLAY!
NOT NOW!
I THINK HE'S INTERESTING.
NO ME GUSTAN LOS ROBOTS.
HE SAYS HE DOESN'T LIKE ROBOTS!
HE'S VERY CUTE!
ROBOTS MAKE ME NERVOUS!

SINCE THE INTRODUCTION DID NOT GO WELL, MUS AND WAGNER TOOK ME TO SEE SLIME, WHO WAS THE OLDEST AND WISEST ANIMAL IN THE FOREST.

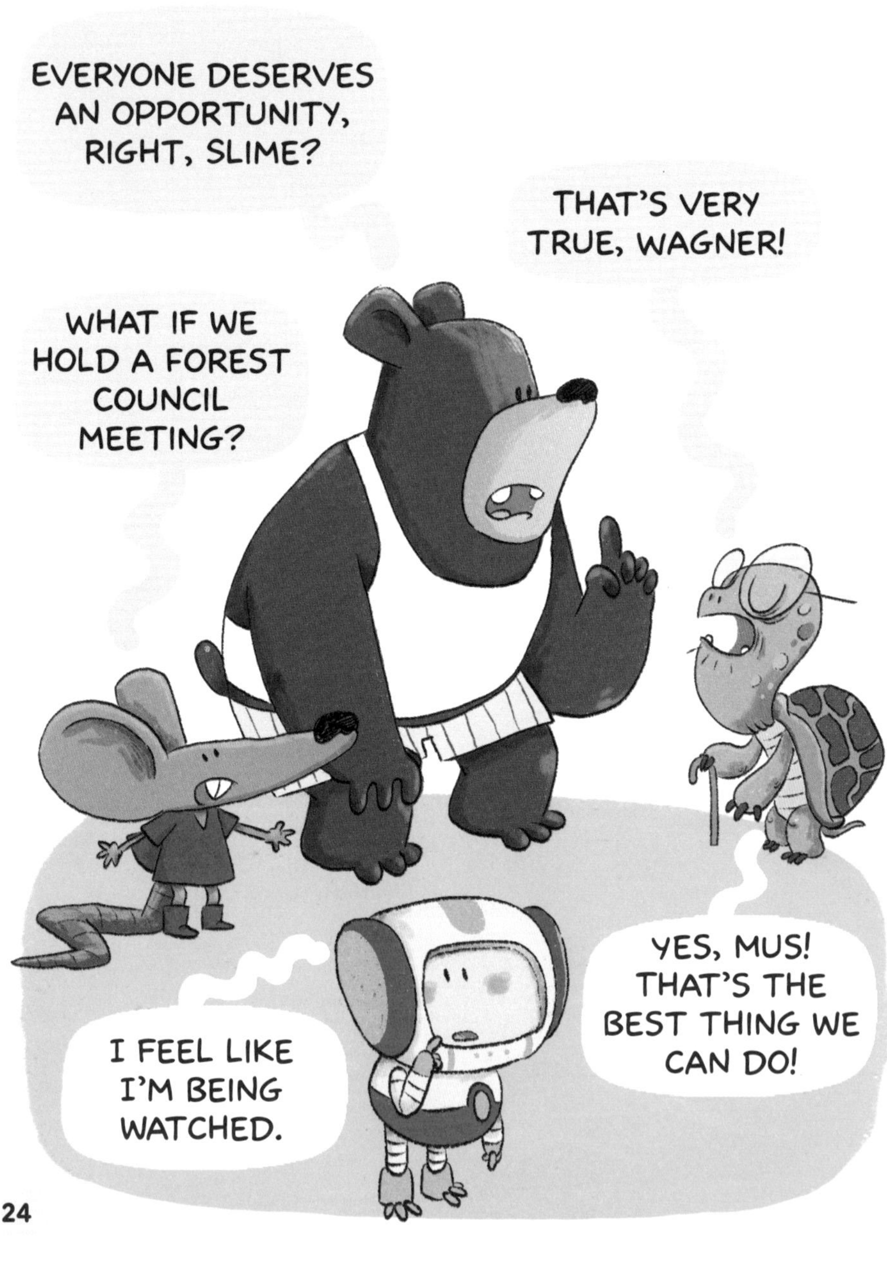
EVERYONE DESERVES AN OPPORTUNITY, RIGHT, SLIME?
THAT'S VERY TRUE, WAGNER!
WHAT IF WE HOLD A FOREST COUNCIL MEETING?
YES, MUS! THAT'S THE BEST THING WE CAN DO!
I FEEL LIKE I'M BEING WATCHED.

THE FOREST COUNCIL

THAT NIGHT THERE WAS A COUNCIL MEETING. MUS, WAGNER, AND I WERE THE FIRST TO ARRIVE.

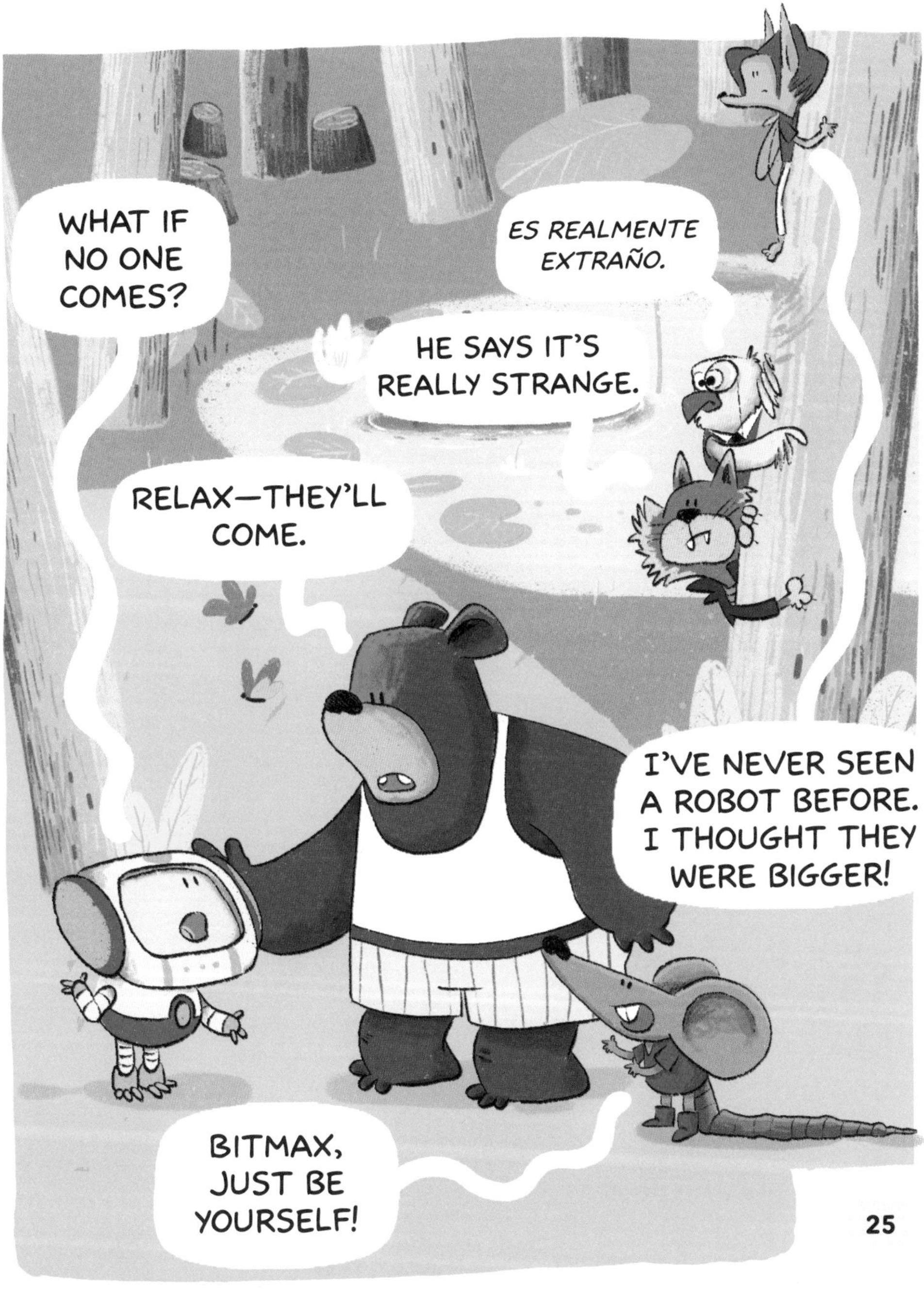
WHAT IF NO ONE COMES?
ES REALMENTE EXTRAÑO.
HE SAYS IT'S REALLY STRANGE.
RELAX—THEY'LL COME.
I'VE NEVER SEEN A ROBOT BEFORE. I THOUGHT THEY WERE BIGGER!
BITMAX, JUST BE YOURSELF!

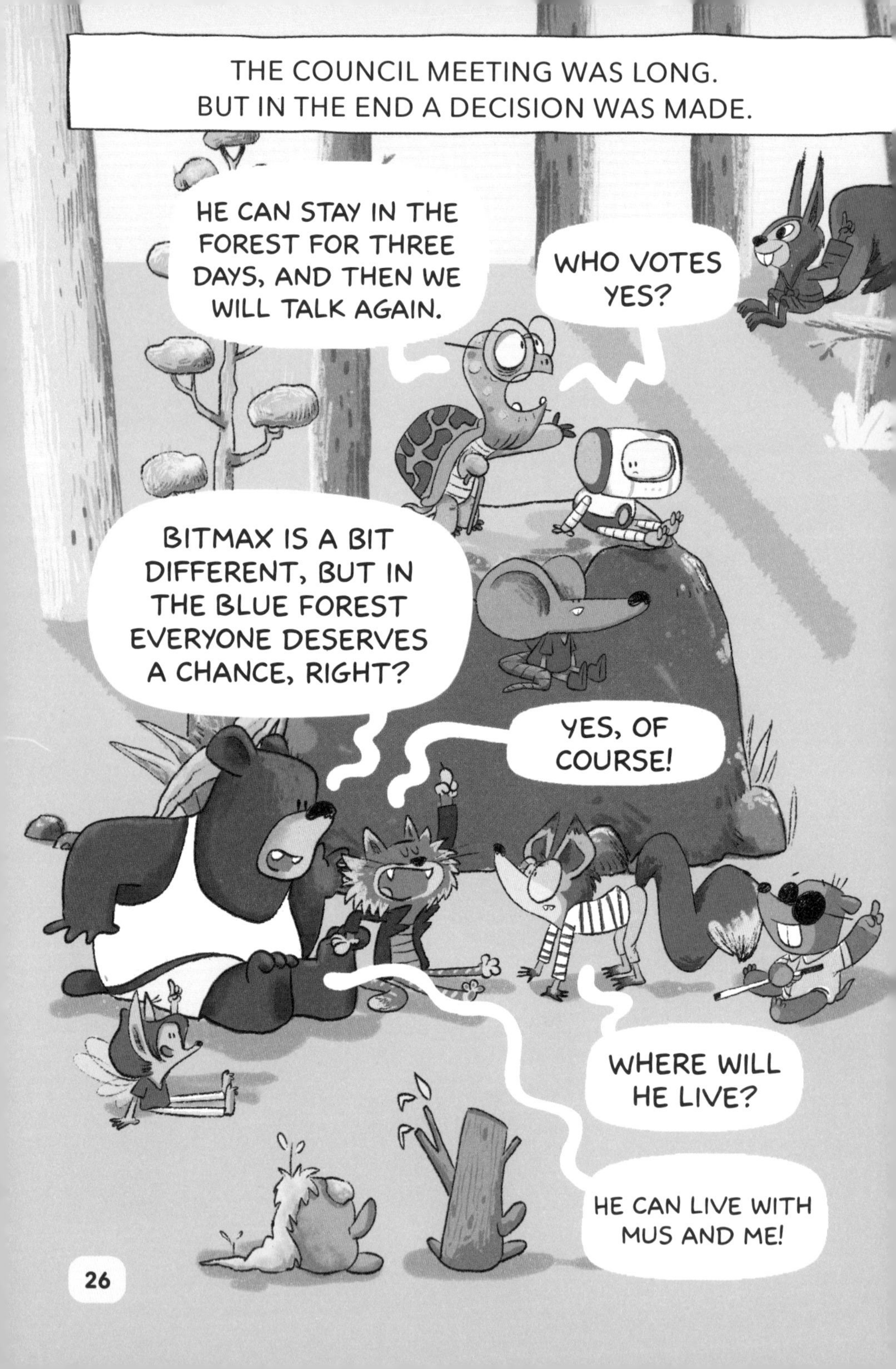
THE COUNCIL MEETING WAS LONG. BUT IN THE END A DECISION WAS MADE.
HE CAN STAY IN THE FOREST FOR THREE DAYS, AND THEN WE WILL TALK AGAIN.
WHO VOTES YES?
BITMAX IS A BIT DIFFERENT, BUT IN THE BLUE FOREST EVERYONE DESERVES A CHANCE, RIGHT?
YES, OF COURSE!
WHERE WILL HE LIVE?
HE CAN LIVE WITH MUS AND ME!

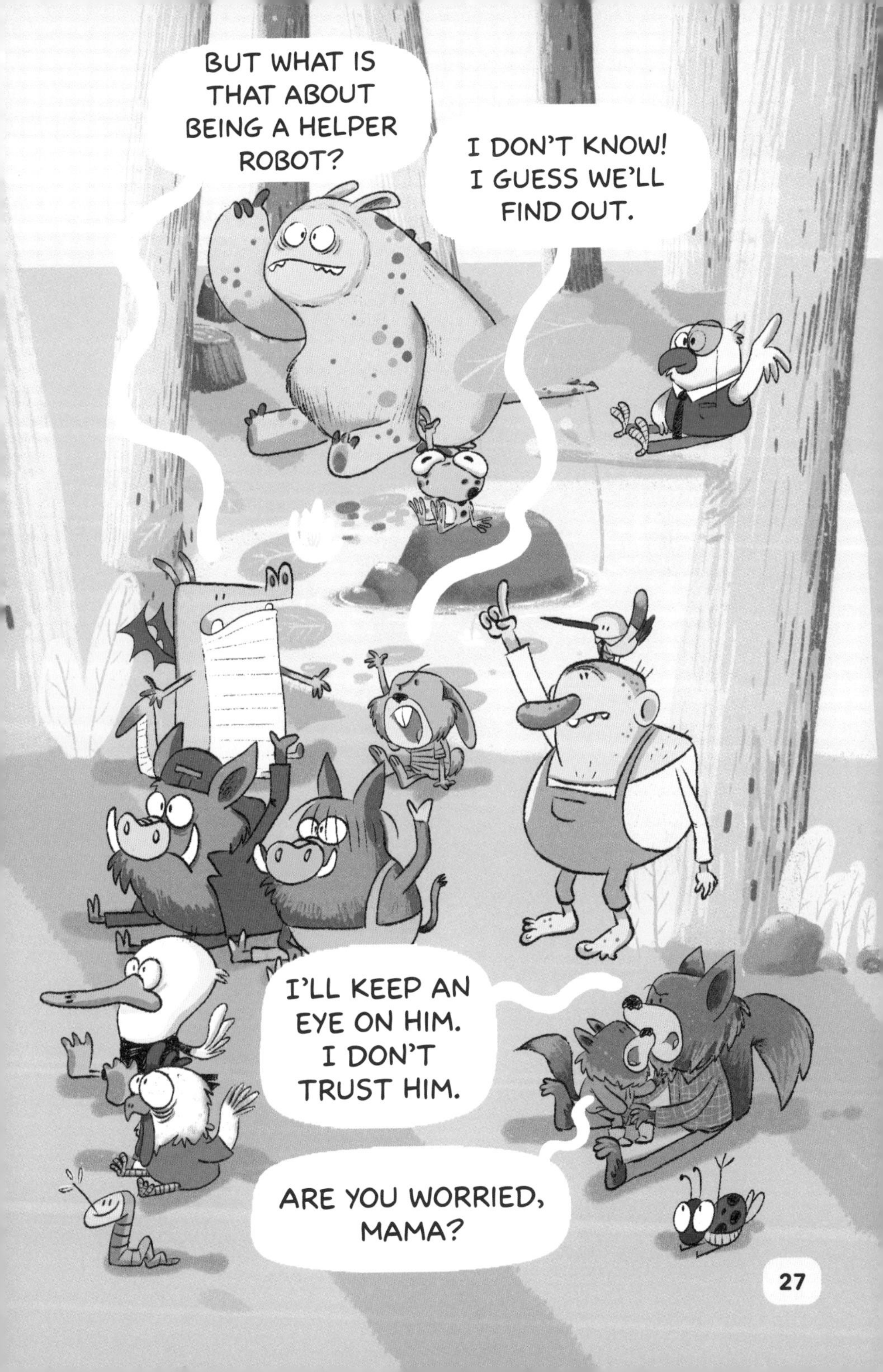
BUT WHAT IS THAT ABOUT BEING A HELPER ROBOT?
I DON'T KNOW! I GUESS WE'LL FIND OUT.
I'LL KEEP AN EYE ON HIM. I DON'T TRUST HIM.
ARE YOU WORRIED, MAMA?

AFTER THE COUNCIL'S DECISION, MUS, WAGNER, AND I CELEBRATED WITH A DRINK OF WATER FROM THE RIVER.

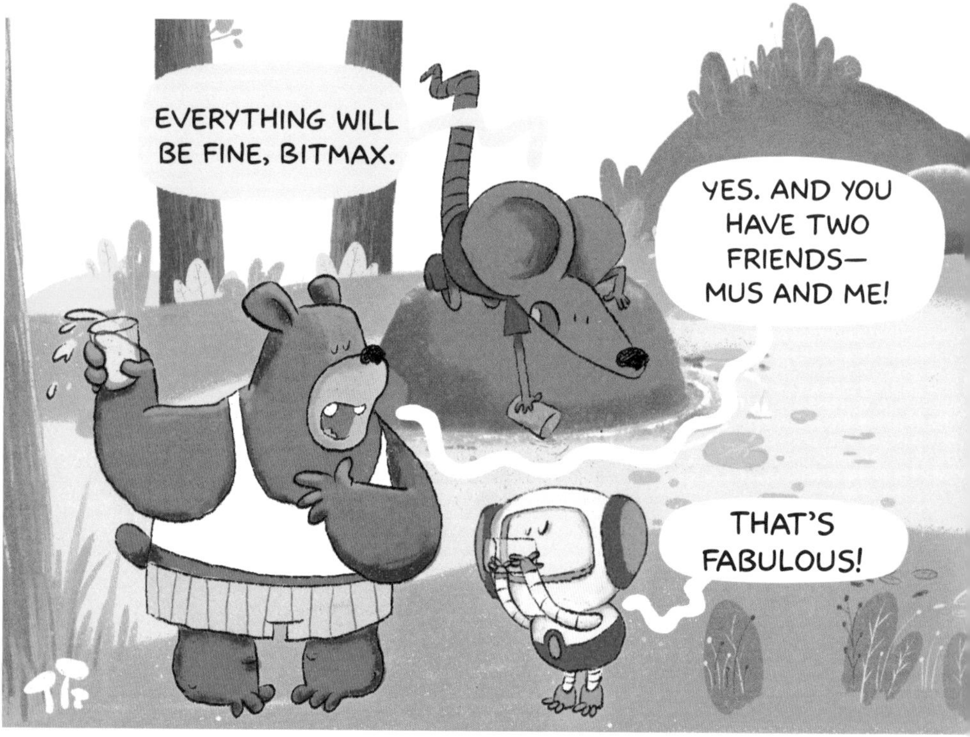
EVERYTHING WILL BE FINE, BITMAX.
YES. AND YOU HAVE TWO FRIENDS—MUS AND ME!
THAT'S FABULOUS!

BUT SUDDENLY . . .

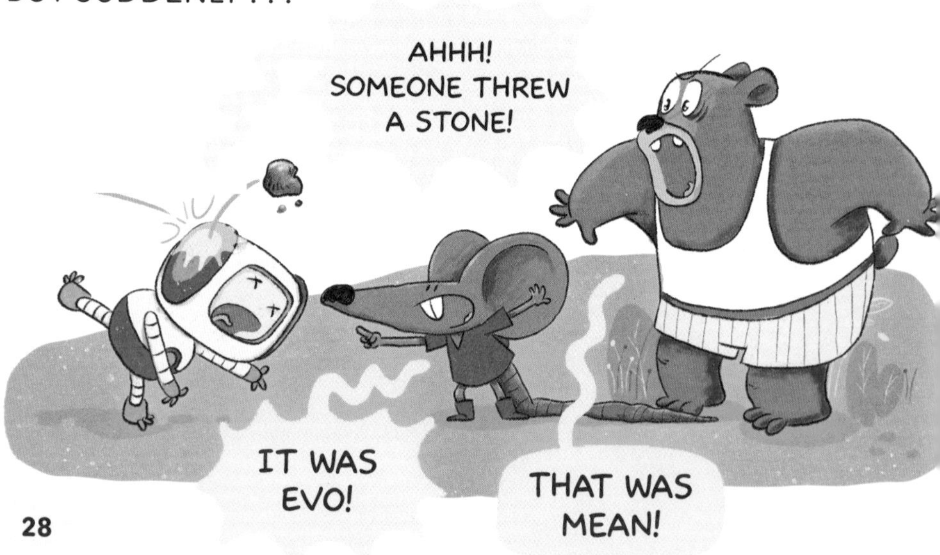
AHHH! SOMEONE THREW A STONE!
IT WAS EVO!
THAT WAS MEAN!

EVO WAS UPSET AND KEPT THROWING STONES AT US.

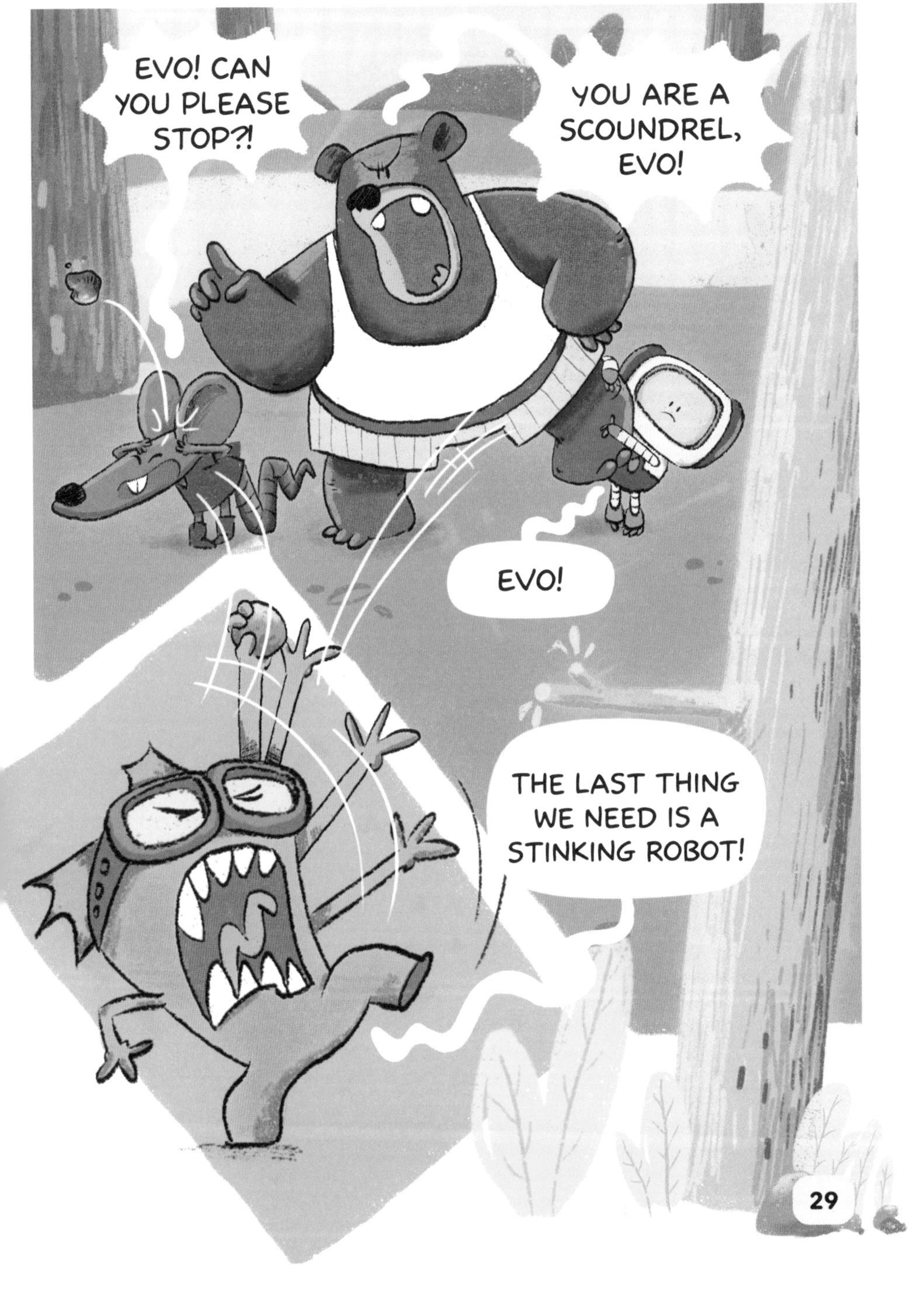
EVO! CAN YOU PLEASE STOP?!
YOU ARE A SCOUNDREL, EVO!
EVO!
THE LAST THING WE NEED IS A STINKING ROBOT!

WHEN EVO LEFT, MUS AND WAGNER EXPLAINED WHO HE WAS.

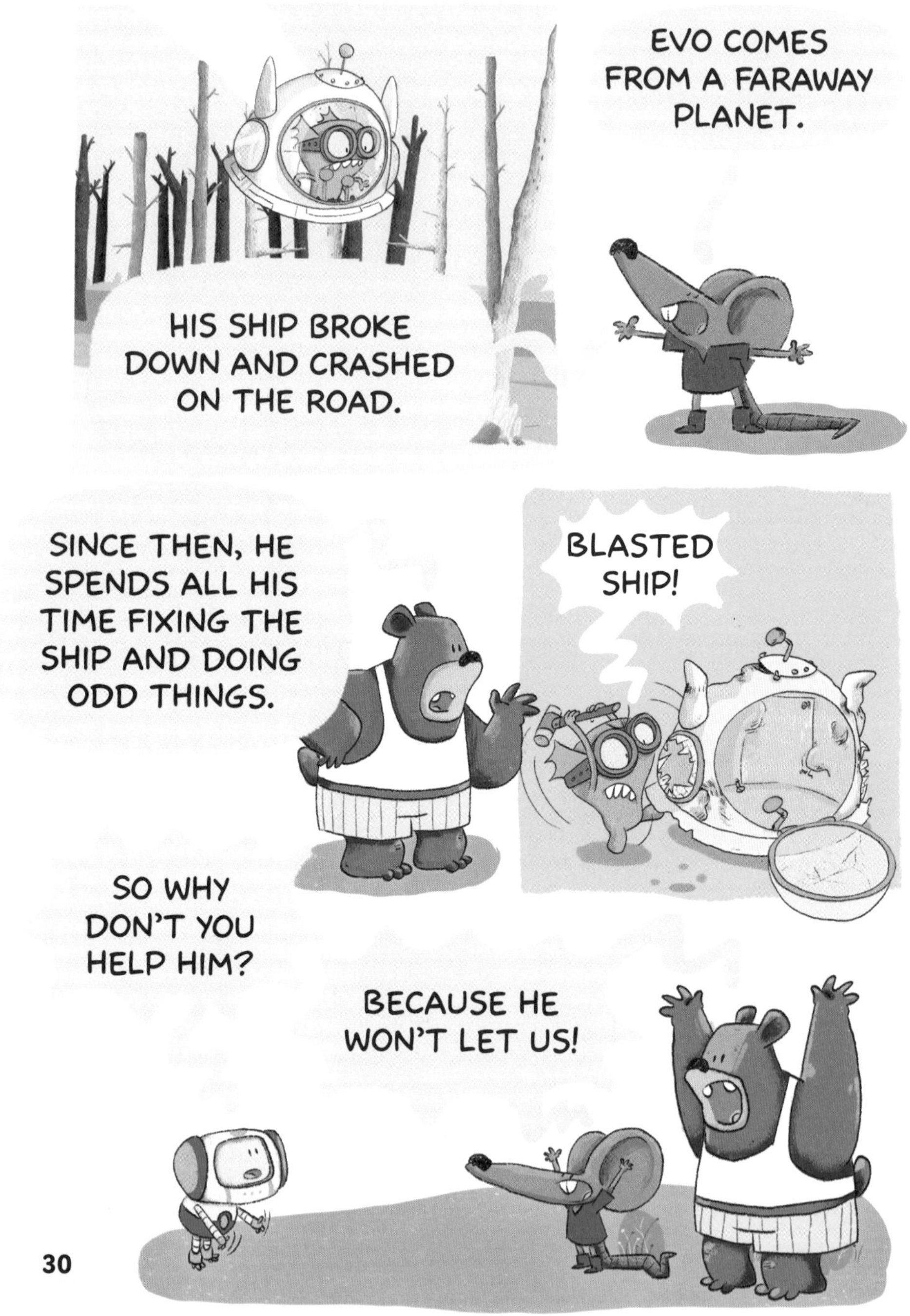
EVO COMES FROM A FARAWAY PLANET.
HIS SHIP BROKE DOWN AND CRASHED ON THE ROAD.
SINCE THEN, HE SPENDS ALL HIS TIME FIXING THE SHIP AND DOING ODD THINGS.
BLASTED SHIP!
SO WHY DON'T YOU HELP HIM?
BECAUSE HE WON'T LET US!

LATER, I SAW WITH MY OWN EYES THAT EVO REALLY DIDN'T WANT ANYONE'S HELP.

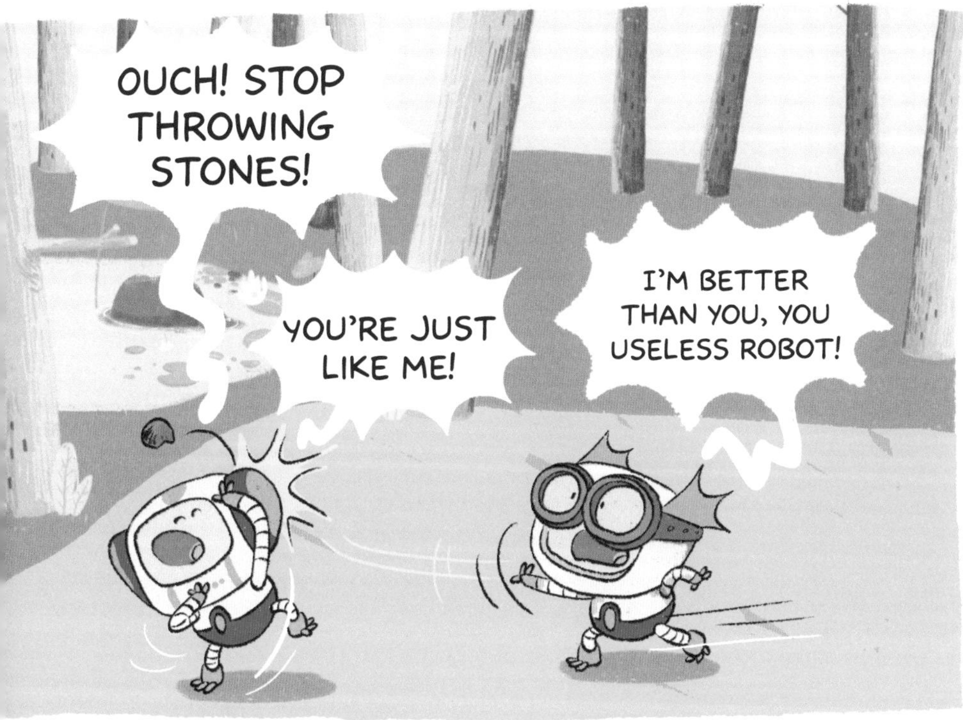
OUCH! STOP THROWING STONES!
YOU'RE JUST LIKE ME!
I'M BETTER THAN YOU, YOU USELESS ROBOT!

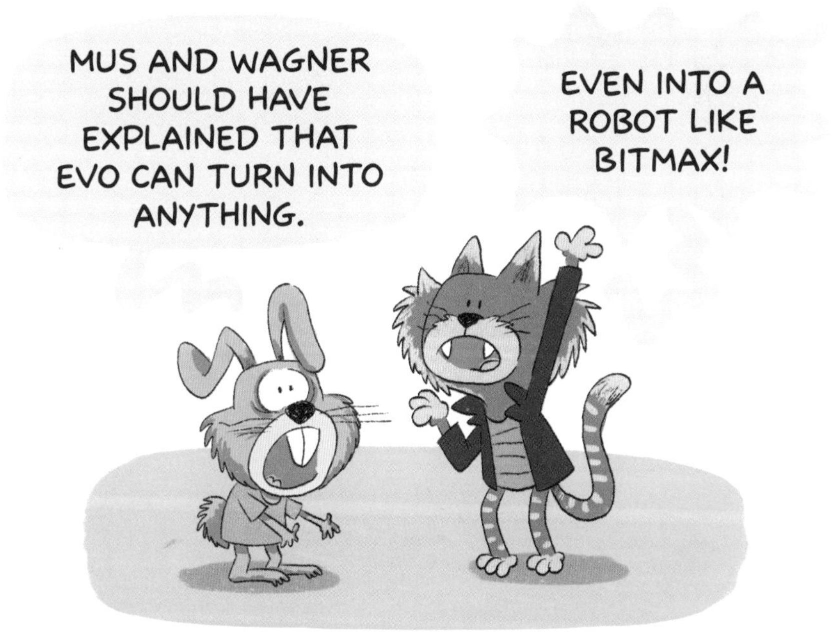
MUS AND WAGNER SHOULD HAVE EXPLAINED THAT EVO CAN TURN INTO ANYTHING.
EVEN INTO A ROBOT LIKE BITMAX!

PART THREE

IN THE FOREST

MY FIRST DAY IN THE FOREST WAS FANTASTIC.

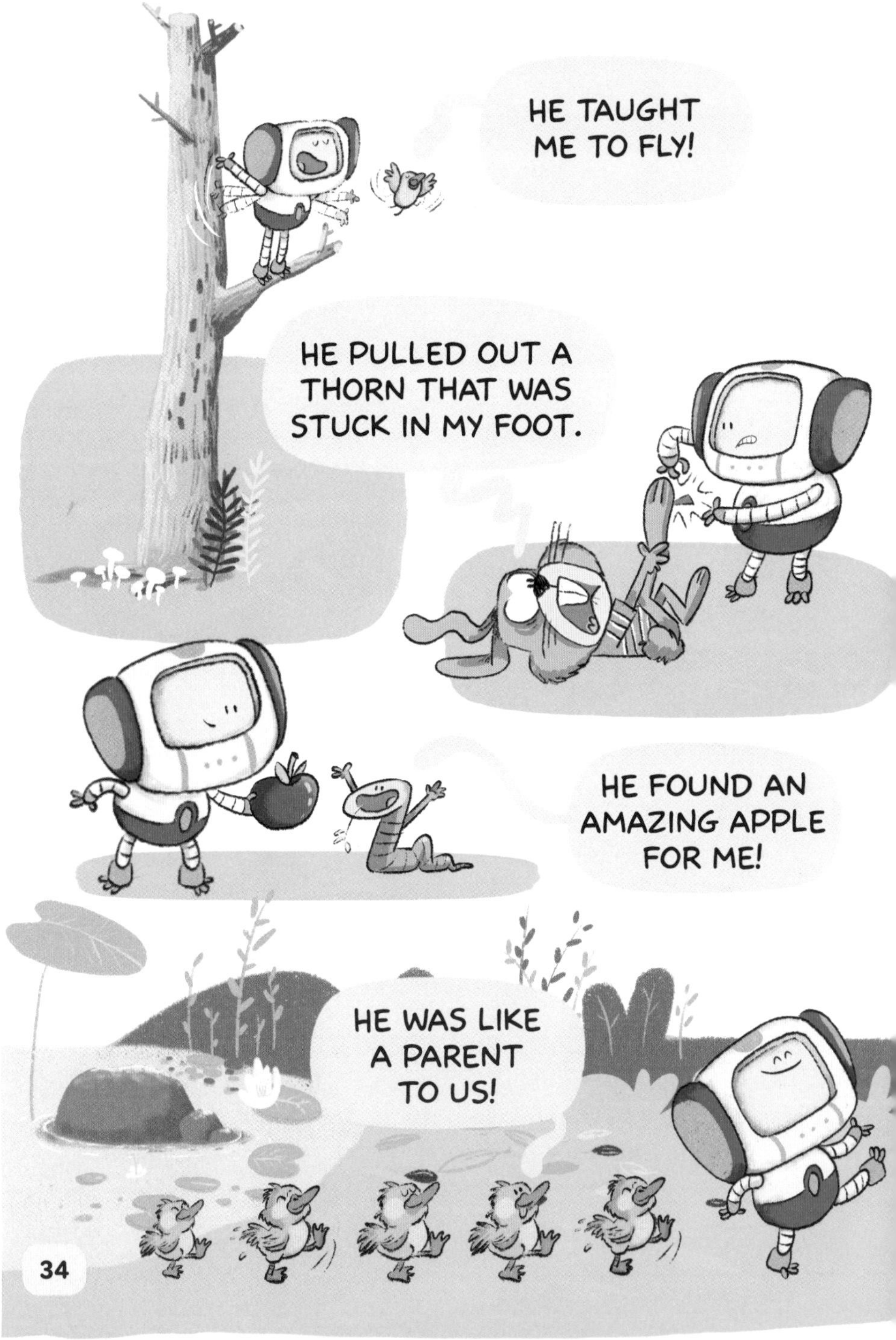
HE TAUGHT ME TO FLY!
HE PULLED OUT A THORN THAT WAS STUCK IN MY FOOT.
HE FOUND AN AMAZING APPLE FOR ME!
HE WAS LIKE A PARENT TO US!

HE HELPED ME COLLECT ACORNS.

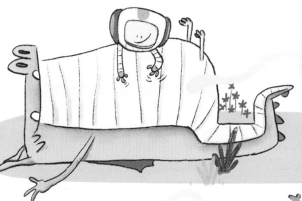

HE SCRATCHED MY BELLY!

HE ENLARGED MY BURROW!

AND AS WELL AS HELPING . . .

. . . HE ALSO MET LOTS OF CREATURES.

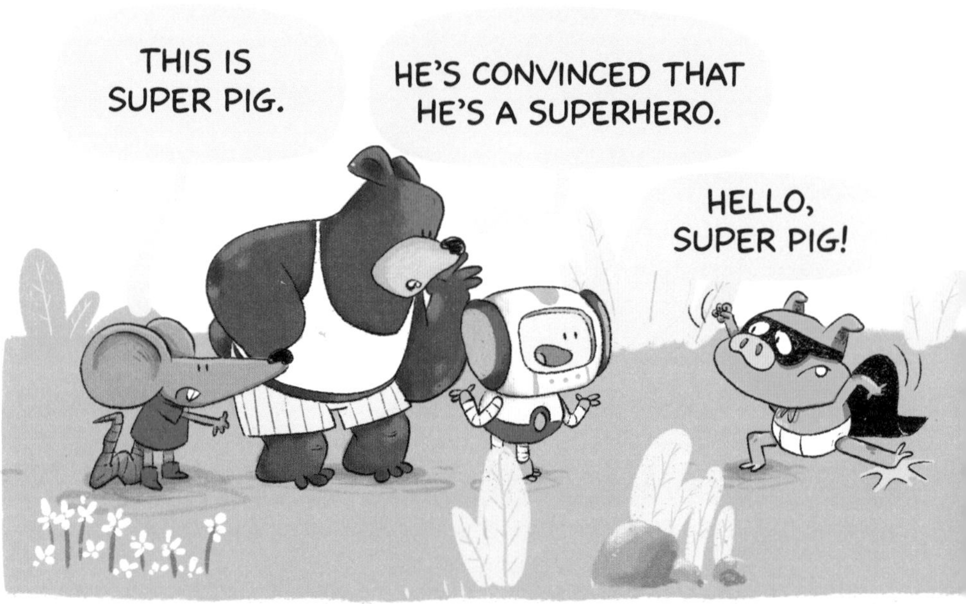
THIS IS SUPER PIG.
HE'S CONVINCED THAT HE'S A SUPERHERO.
HELLO, SUPER PIG!

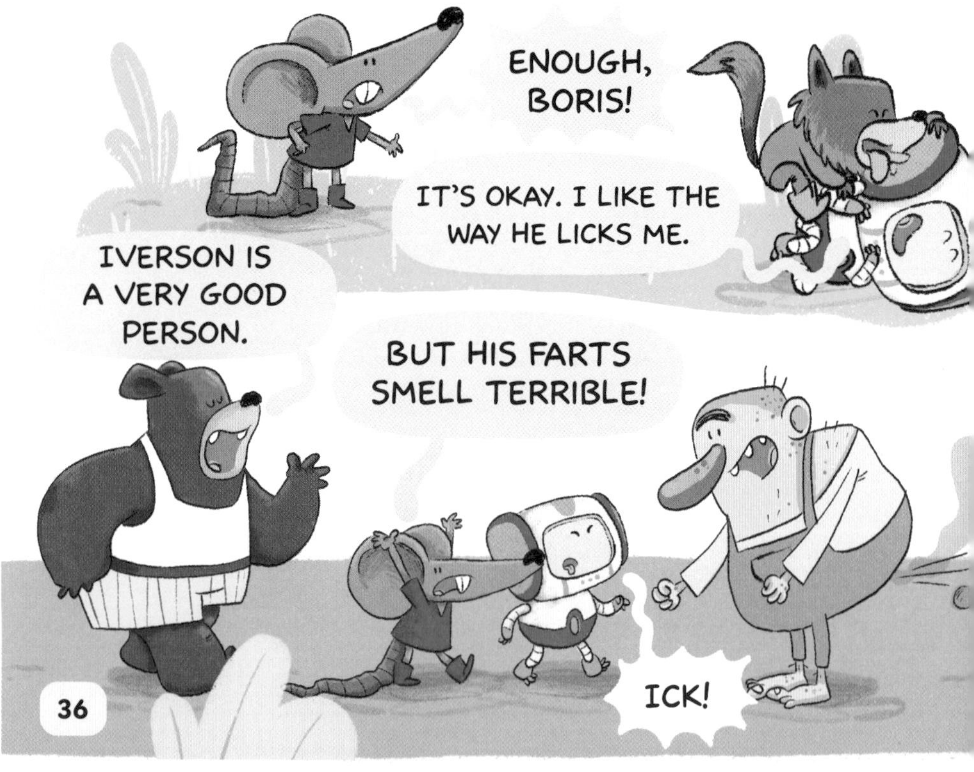
ENOUGH, BORIS!
IT'S OKAY. I LIKE THE WAY HE LICKS ME.
IVERSON IS A VERY GOOD PERSON.
BUT HIS FARTS SMELL TERRIBLE!
ICK!

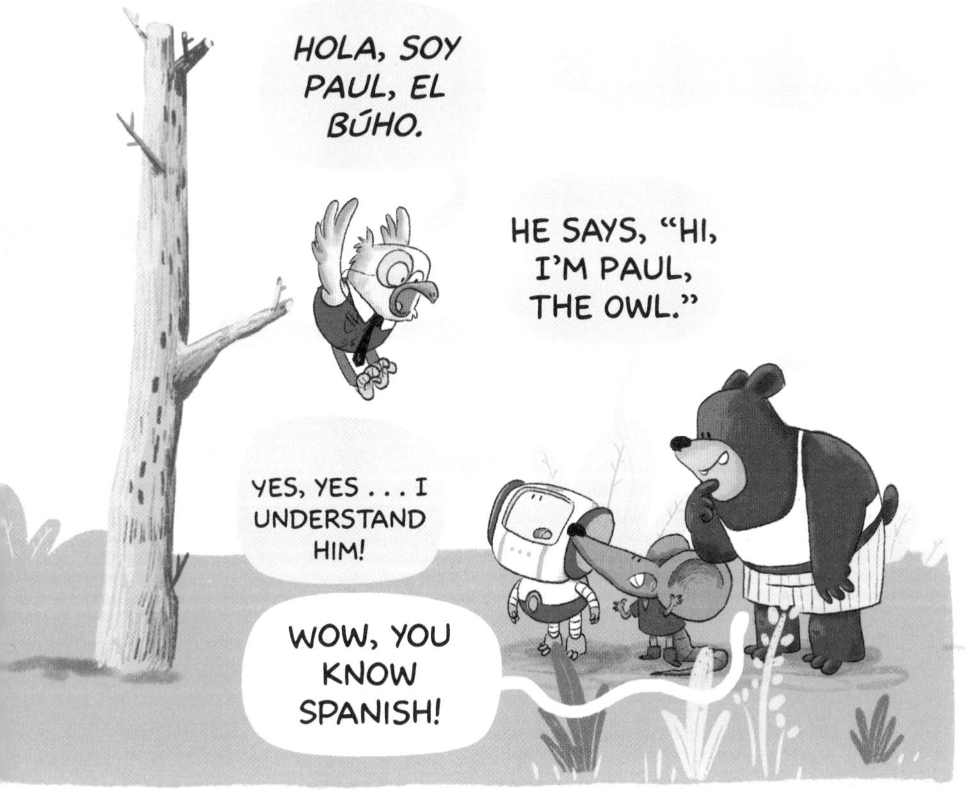
HOLA, SOY PAUL, EL BÚHO.
HE SAYS, "HI, I'M PAUL, THE OWL."
YES, YES . . . I UNDERSTAND HIM!
WOW, YOU KNOW SPANISH!

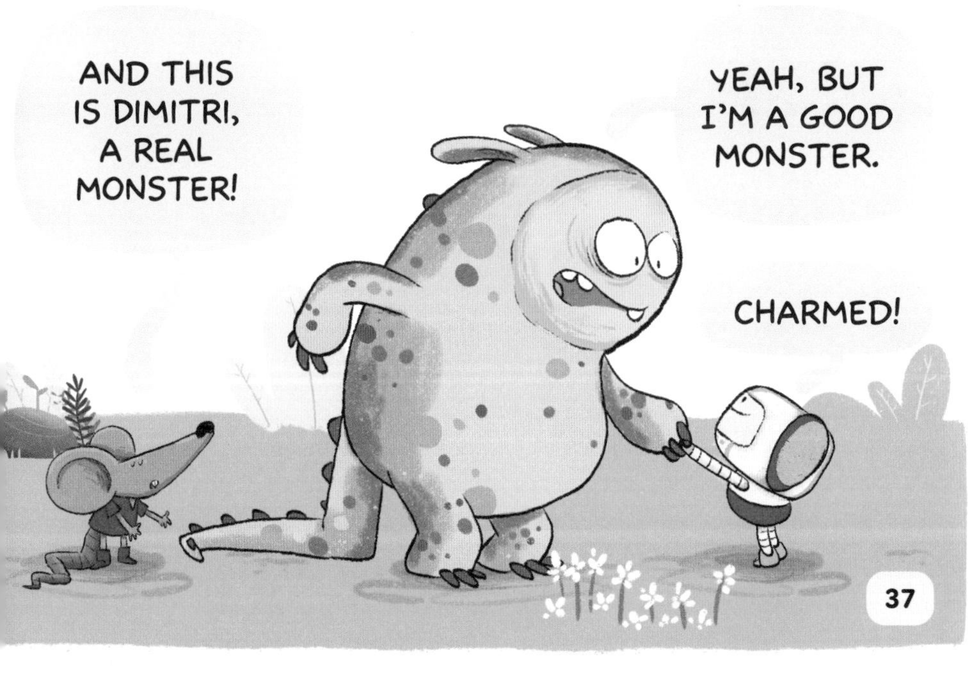
AND THIS IS DIMITRI, A REAL MONSTER!
YEAH, BUT I'M A GOOD MONSTER.
CHARMED!

THAT FIRST DAY WAS PERFECT, BUT IN THE AFTERNOON, WHEN WE WENT TO THE ROCK ON THE ROAD . . .

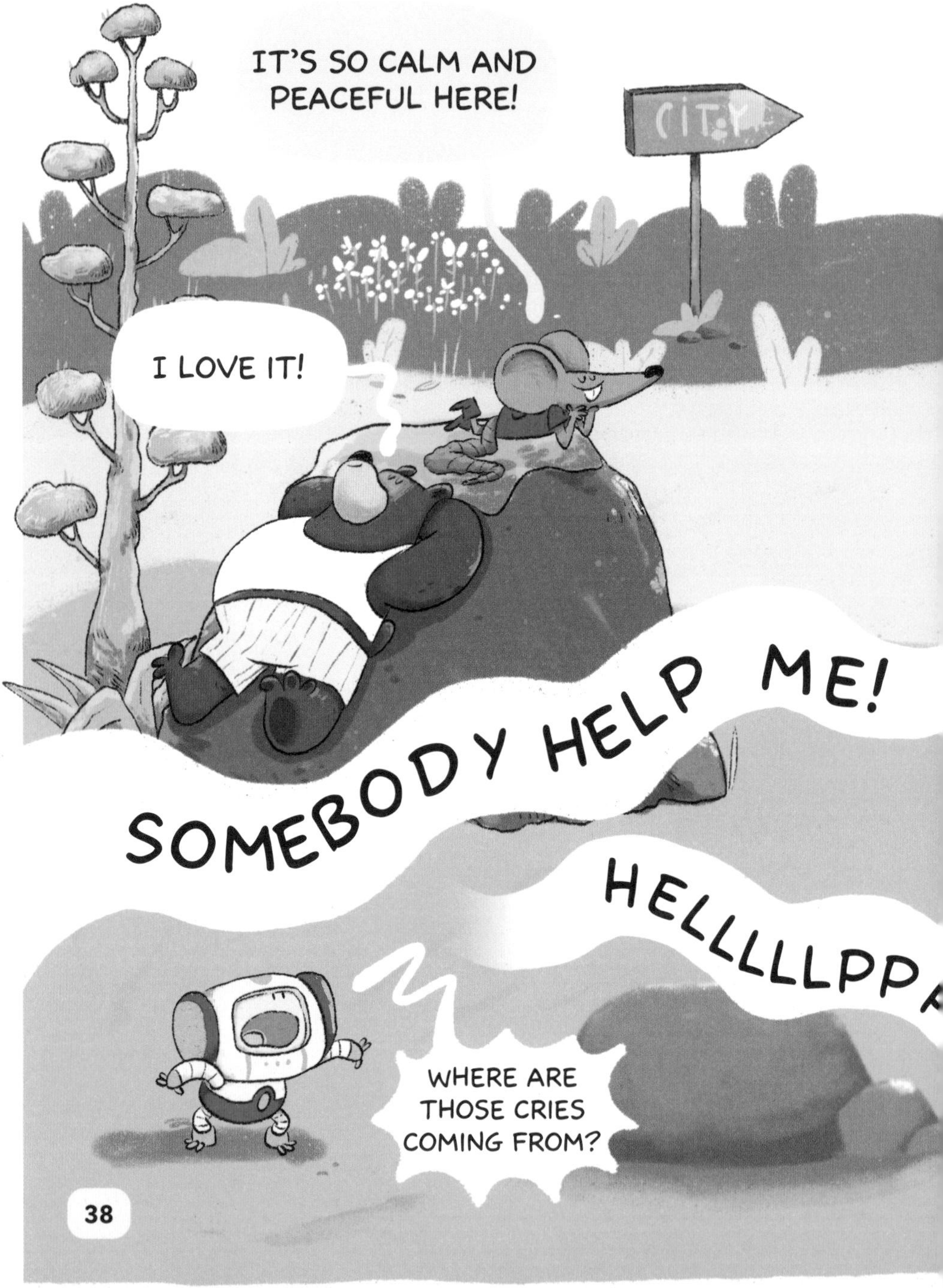
IT'S SO CALM AND PEACEFUL HERE!
CITY
I LOVE IT!
SOMEBODY HELP ME!
HELLLLLPP
WHERE ARE THOSE CRIES COMING FROM?

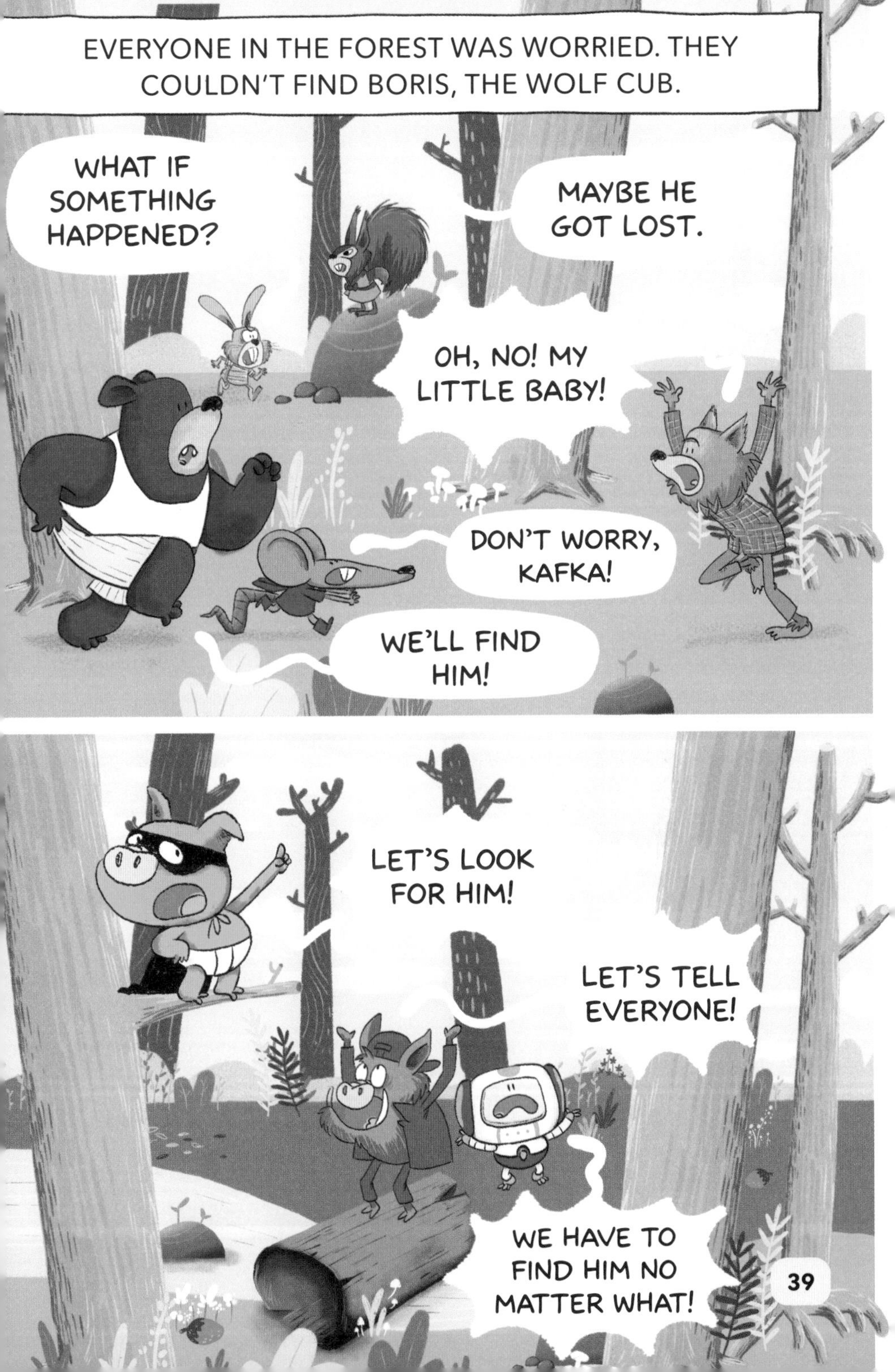
EVERYONE IN THE FOREST WAS WORRIED. THEY COULDN'T FIND BORIS, THE WOLF CUB.
WHAT IF SOMETHING HAPPENED?
MAYBE HE GOT LOST.
OH, NO! MY LITTLE BABY!
DON'T WORRY, KAFKA!
WE'LL FIND HIM!
LET'S LOOK FOR HIM!
LET'S TELL EVERYONE!
WE HAVE TO FIND HIM NO MATTER WHAT!

EVERYONE WAS LOOKING FOR LITTLE BORIS.

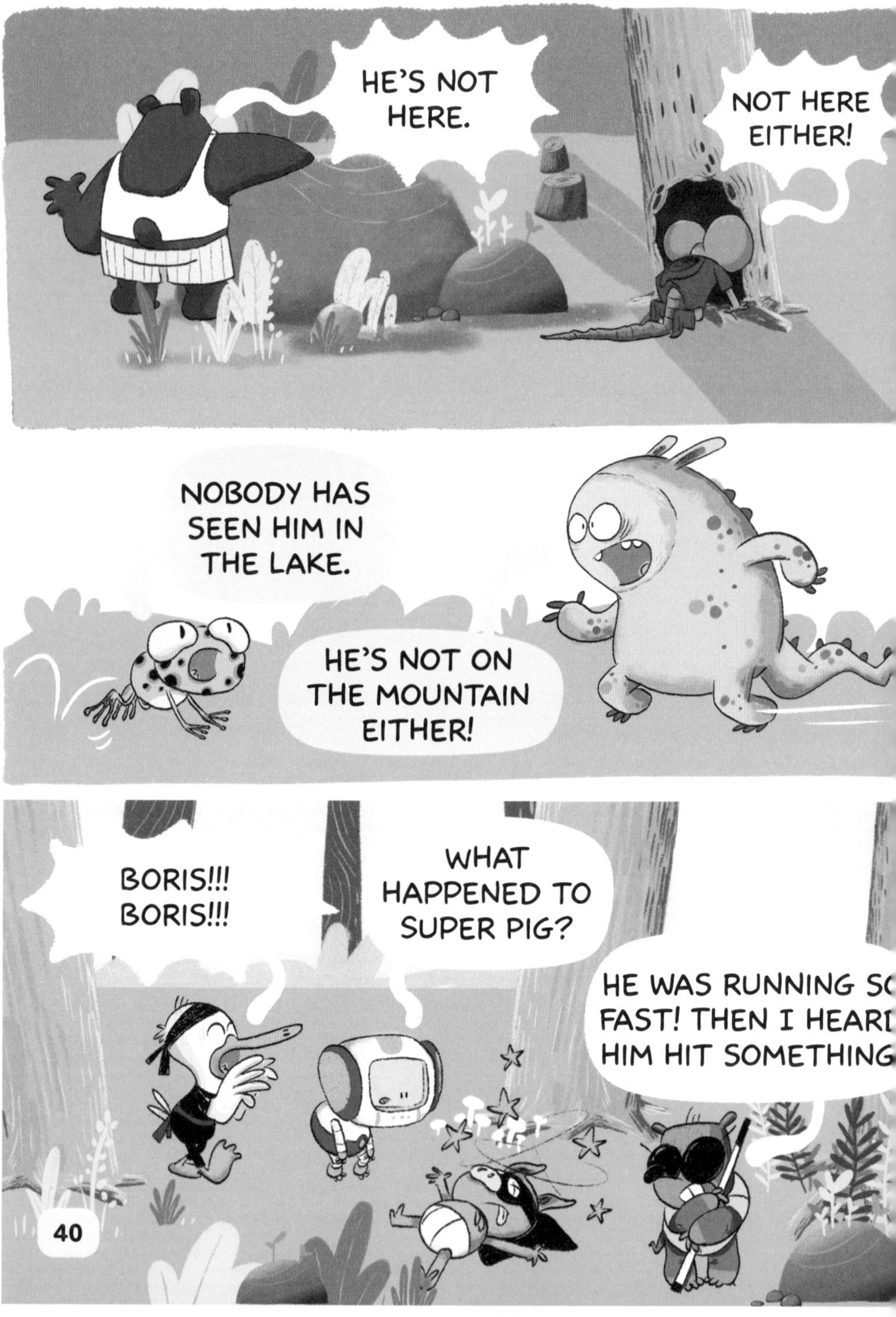
HE'S NOT HERE.
NOT HERE EITHER!
NOBODY HAS SEEN HIM IN THE LAKE.
HE'S NOT ON THE MOUNTAIN EITHER!
BORIS!!! BORIS!!!
WHAT HAPPENED TO SUPER PIG?
HE WAS RUNNING SO FAST! THEN I HEARD HIM HIT SOMETHING

SUDDENLY, SINATRA ARRIVED. HE WAS ON HIS WAY BACK FROM THE CITY, AND HE WAS VERY CONCERNED.

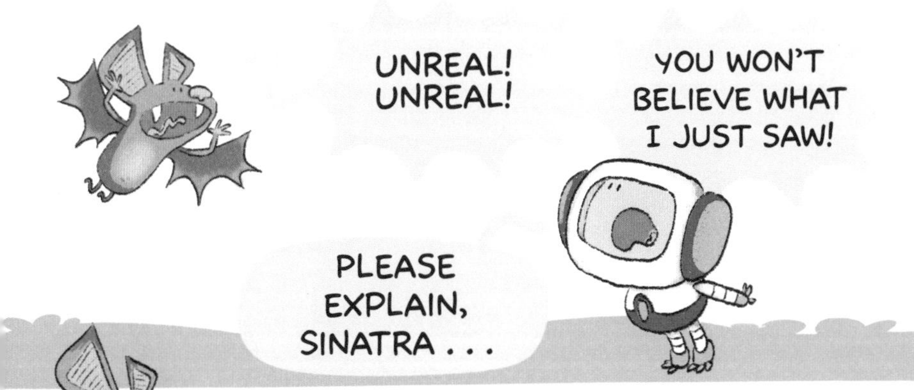
UNREAL!
UNREAL!
YOU WON'T BELIEVE WHAT I JUST SAW!
PLEASE EXPLAIN, SINATRA . . .

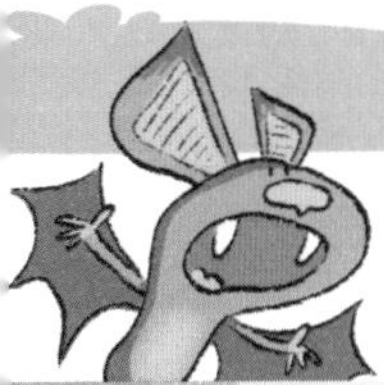

THIS IS WHAT SINATRA SAID:

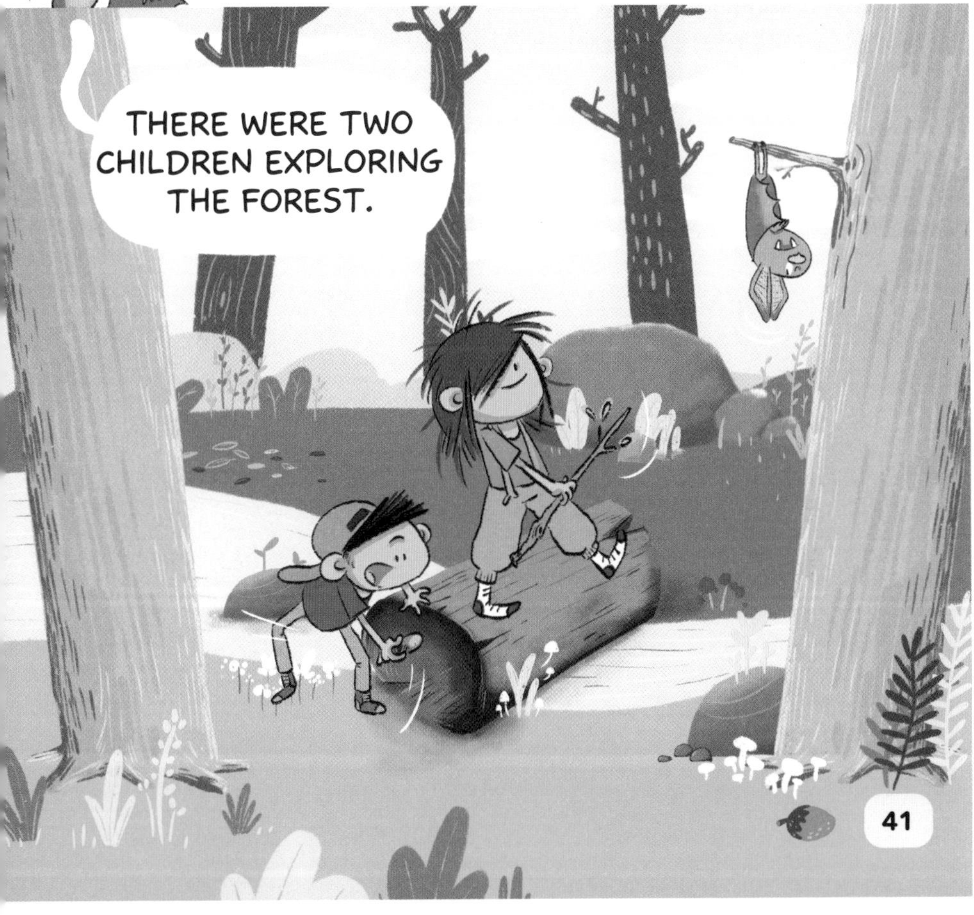
THERE WERE TWO CHILDREN EXPLORING THE FOREST.

SINATRA SAW EVO TURN INTO A SWEET GRANDMOTHER AND TRICK THE CHILDREN INTO TAKING BORIS.

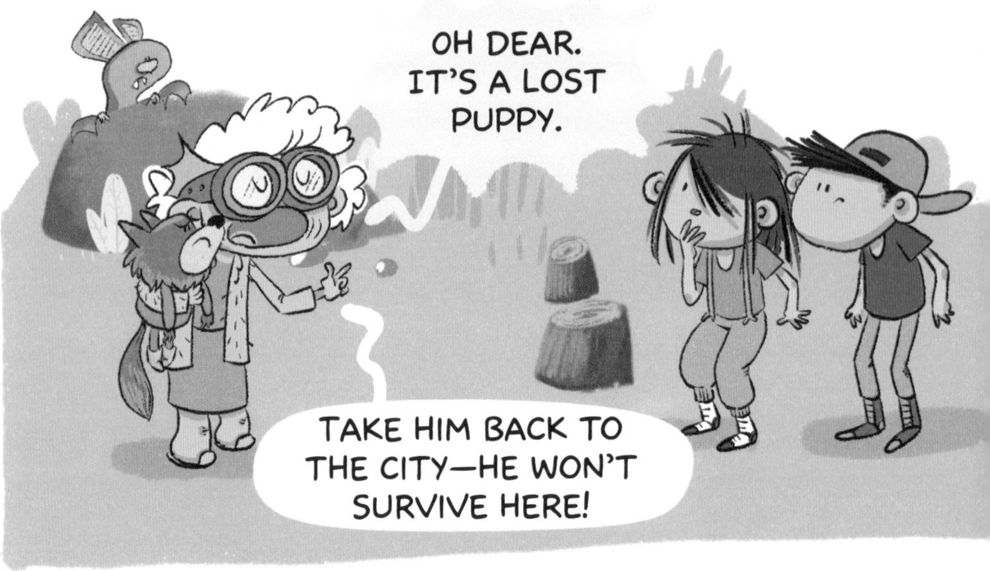
OH DEAR. IT'S A LOST PUPPY.
TAKE HIM BACK TO THE CITY—HE WON'T SURVIVE HERE!

SO THE CHILDREN PICKED UP BORIS AND CARRIED HIM AWAY TO THE CITY.

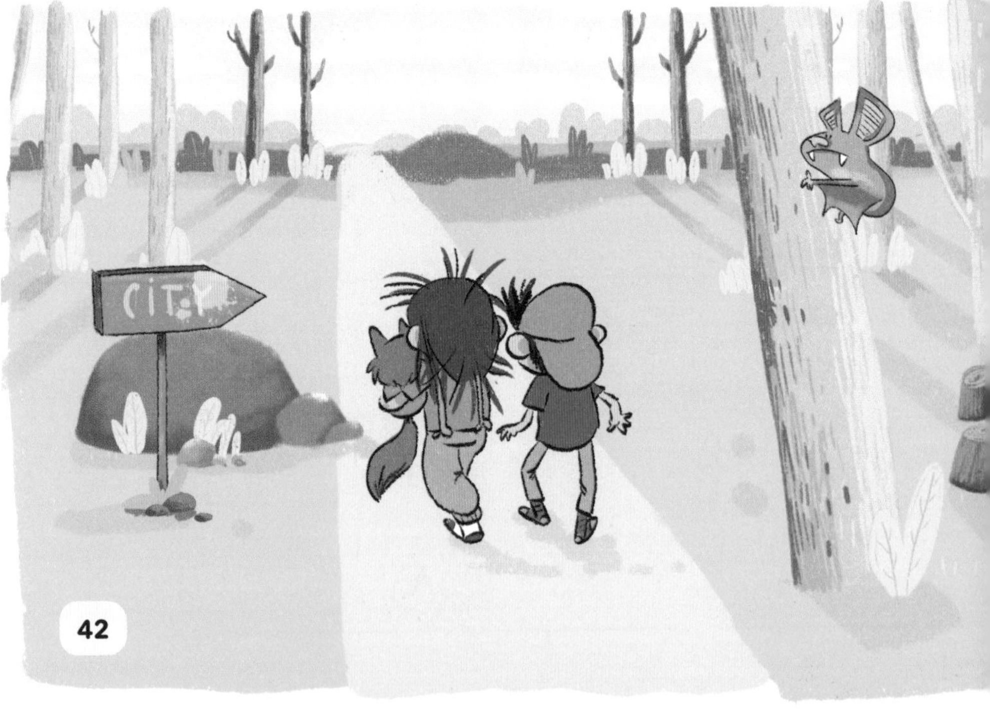
CITY

BUT WHEN THEIR PARENTS SAW BORIS, THEY REALIZED HE WAS A WOLF CUB.

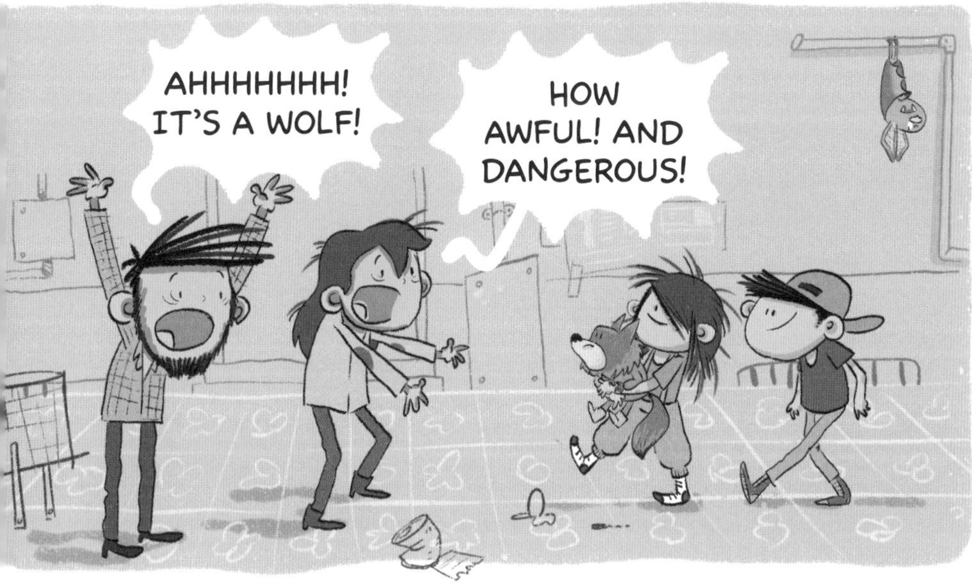
AHHHHHHH! IT'S A WOLF!
HOW AWFUL! AND DANGEROUS!

THE CHILDREN'S PARENTS TOOK BORIS TO THE TOWN HALL. HE WILL STAY THERE UNTIL SOMEONE ARRIVES TO TAKE HIM TO A ZOO.

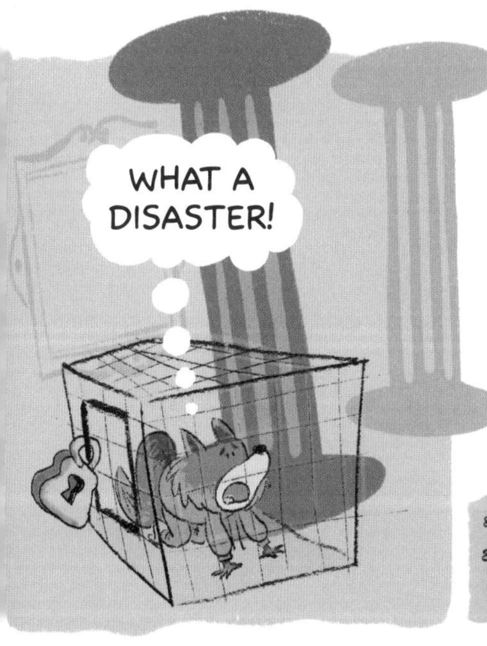
WHAT A DISASTER!

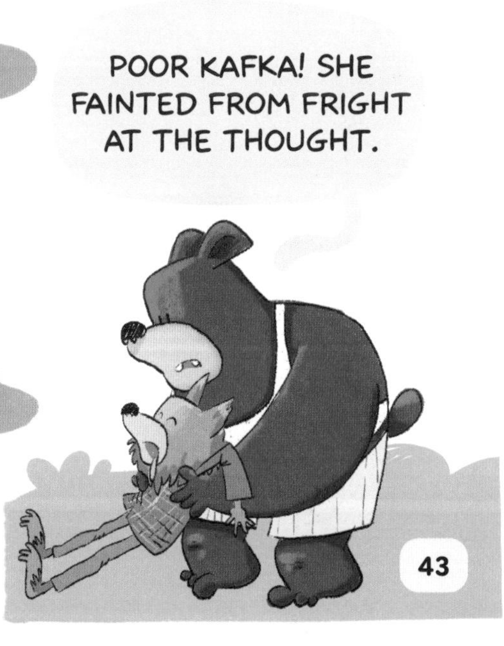
POOR KAFKA! SHE FAINTED FROM FRIGHT AT THE THOUGHT.

SO THEN I MADE A DECISION.

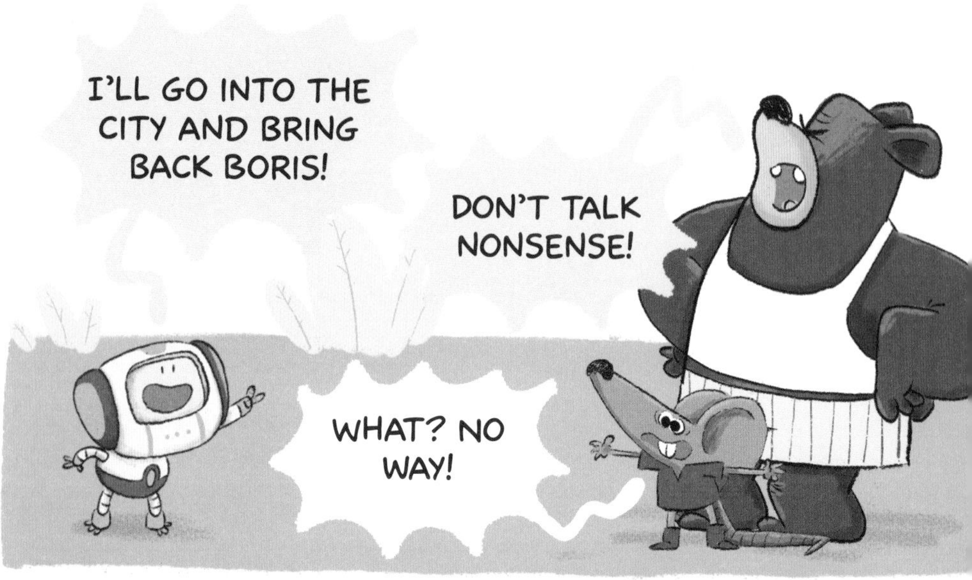
I'LL GO INTO THE CITY AND BRING BACK BORIS!
DON'T TALK NONSENSE!
WHAT? NO WAY!

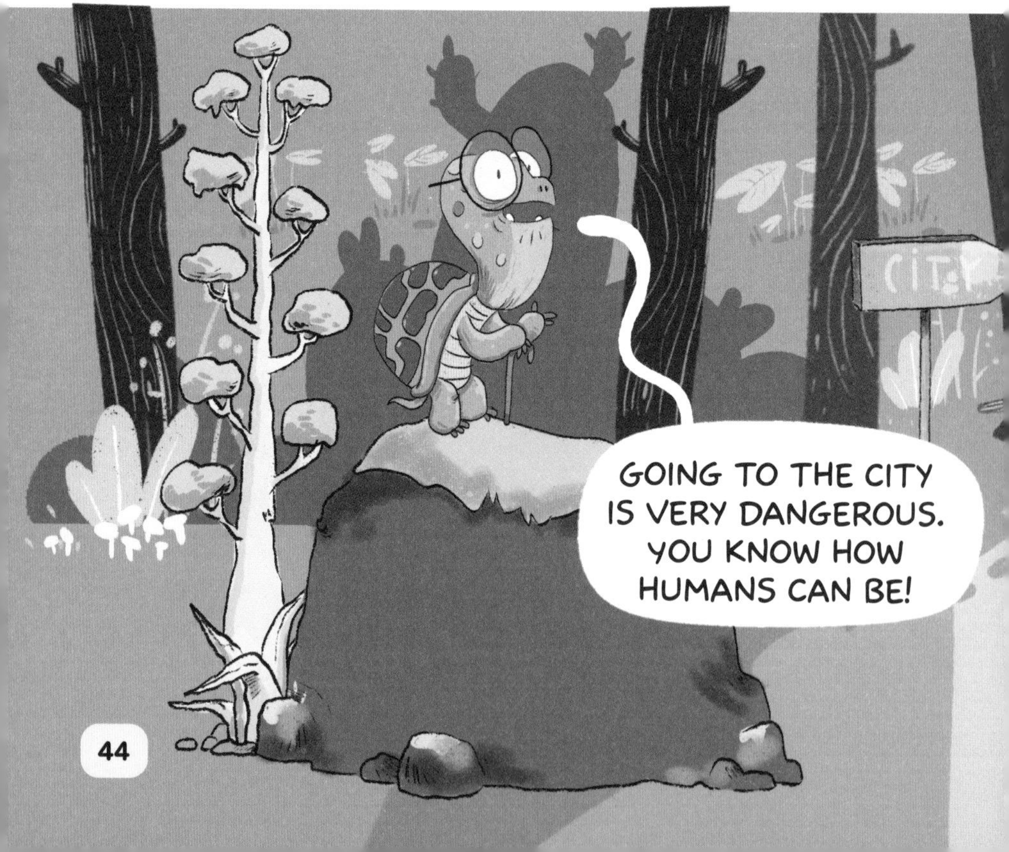
GOING TO THE CITY IS VERY DANGEROUS. YOU KNOW HOW HUMANS CAN BE!

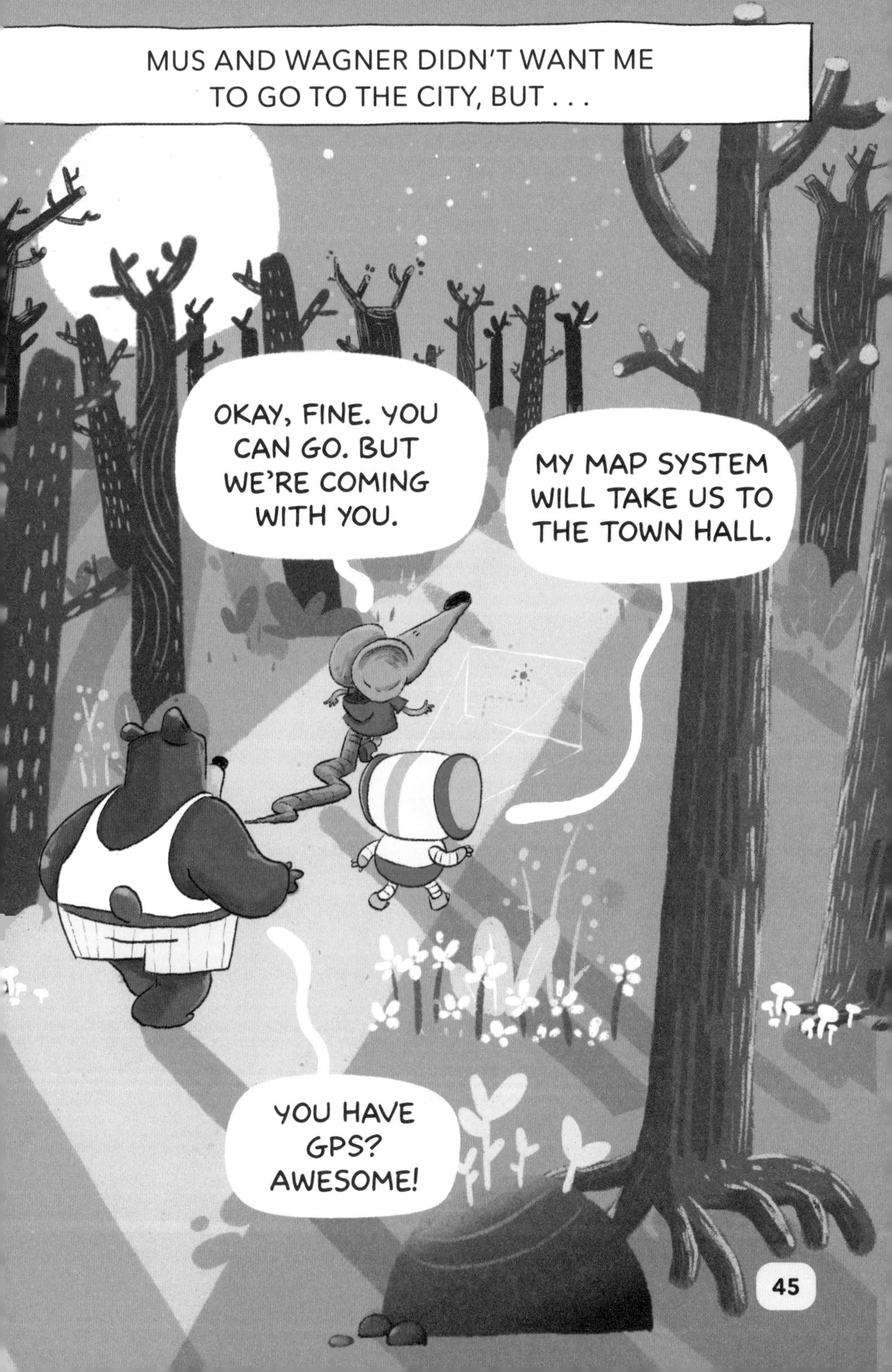
MUS AND WAGNER DIDN'T WANT ME TO GO TO THE CITY, BUT . . .
OKAY, FINE. YOU CAN GO. BUT WE'RE COMING WITH YOU.
MY MAP SYSTEM WILL TAKE US TO THE TOWN HALL.
YOU HAVE GPS? AWESOME!

PART FOUR

THE CITY

WE HAD NO PROBLEM GETTING TO THE TOWN HALL, BUT WE DIDN'T REALIZE THERE WOULD BE A GUARD AT THE DOOR.

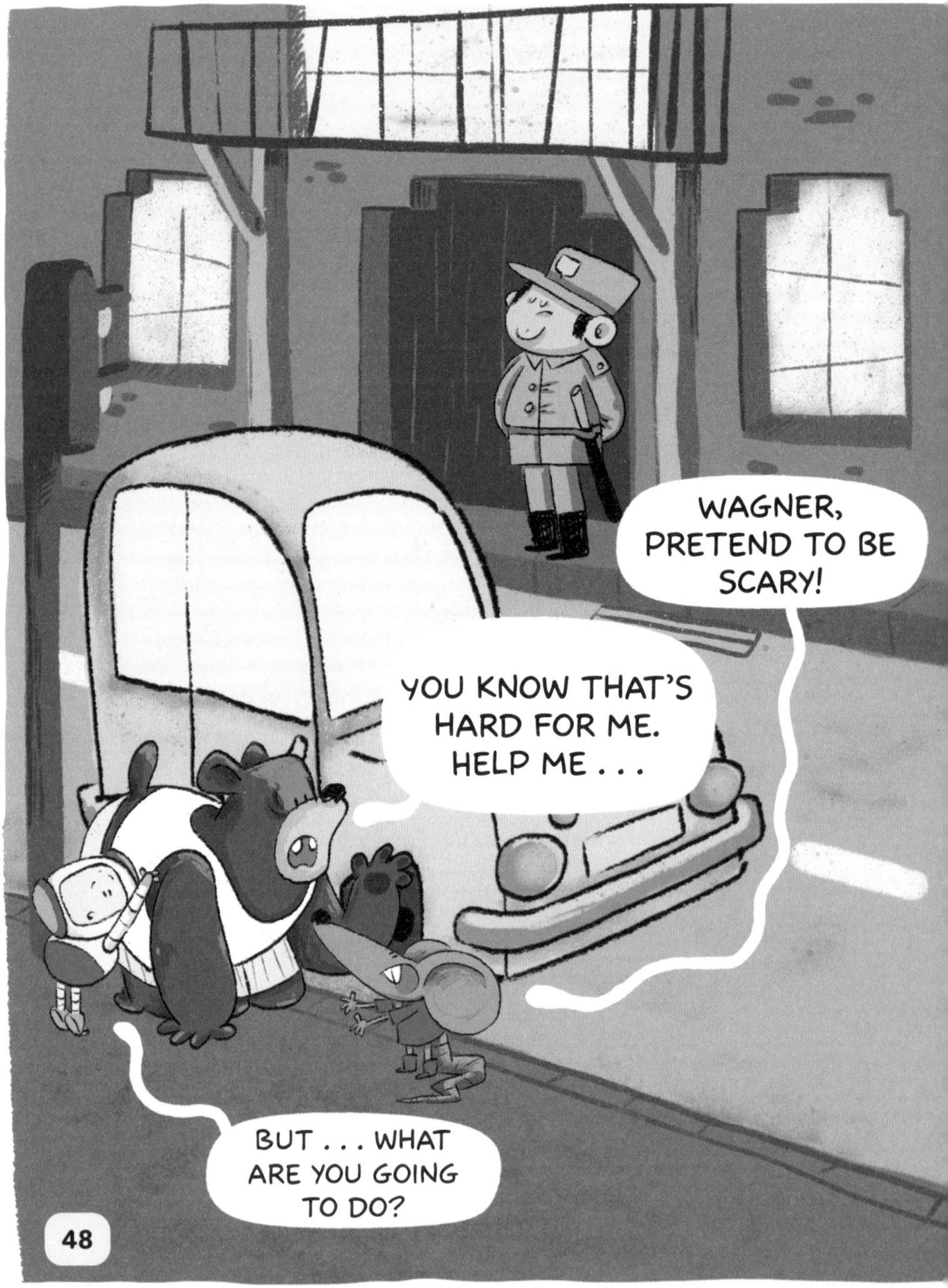
WAGNER, PRETEND TO BE SCARY!
YOU KNOW THAT'S HARD FOR ME. HELP ME . . .
BUT . . . WHAT ARE YOU GOING TO DO?

MUS STARTED SAYING MEAN THINGS TO MAKE WAGNER ANGRY . . .

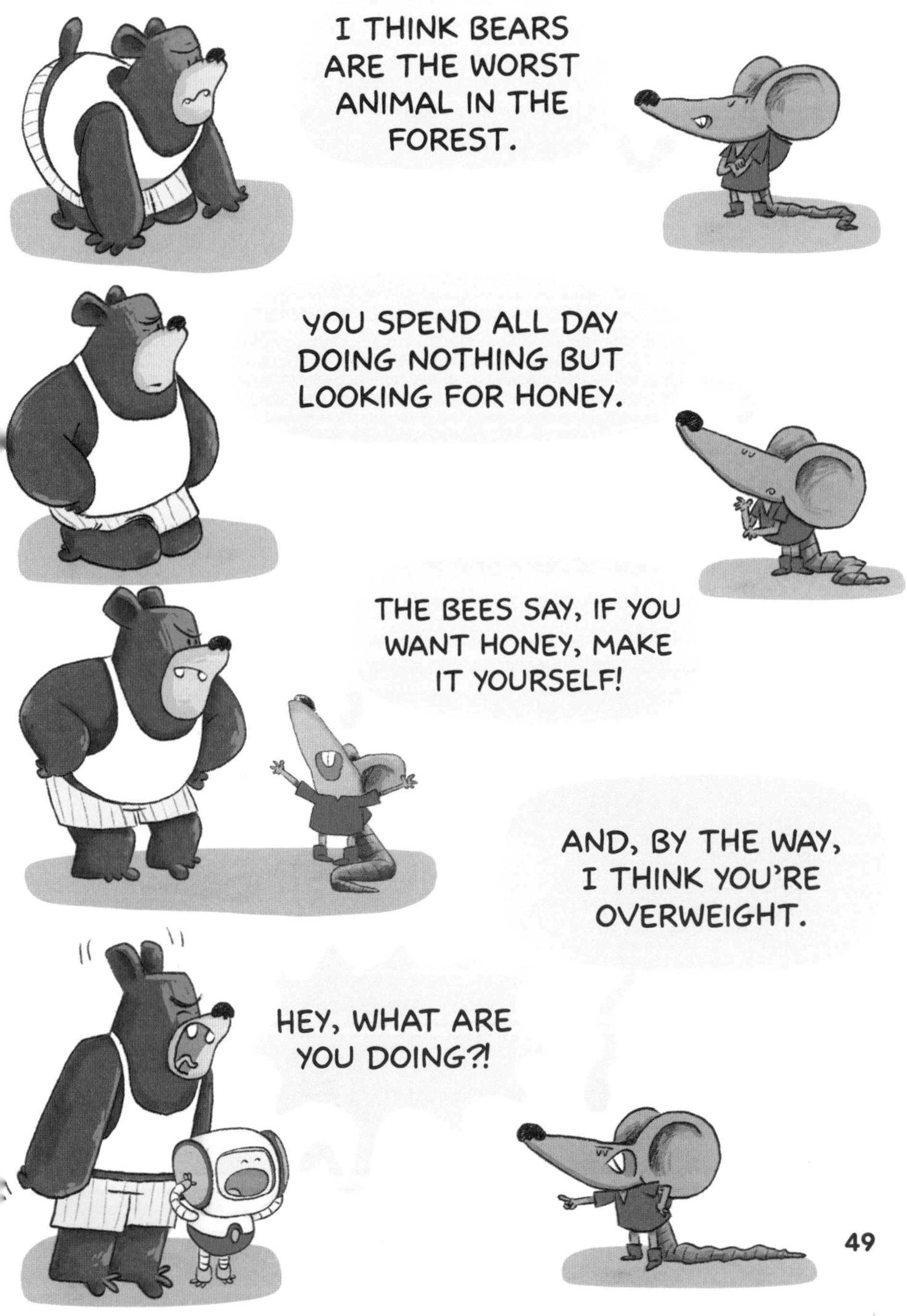
I THINK BEARS ARE THE WORST ANIMAL IN THE FOREST.
YOU SPEND ALL DAY DOING NOTHING BUT LOOKING FOR HONEY.
THE BEES SAY, IF YOU WANT HONEY, MAKE IT YOURSELF!
AND, BY THE WAY, I THINK YOU'RE OVERWEIGHT.
HEY, WHAT ARE YOU DOING?!

AND THEN SUDDENLY, I UNDERSTOOD WHY MUS HAD MAD WAGNER SO ANGRY.

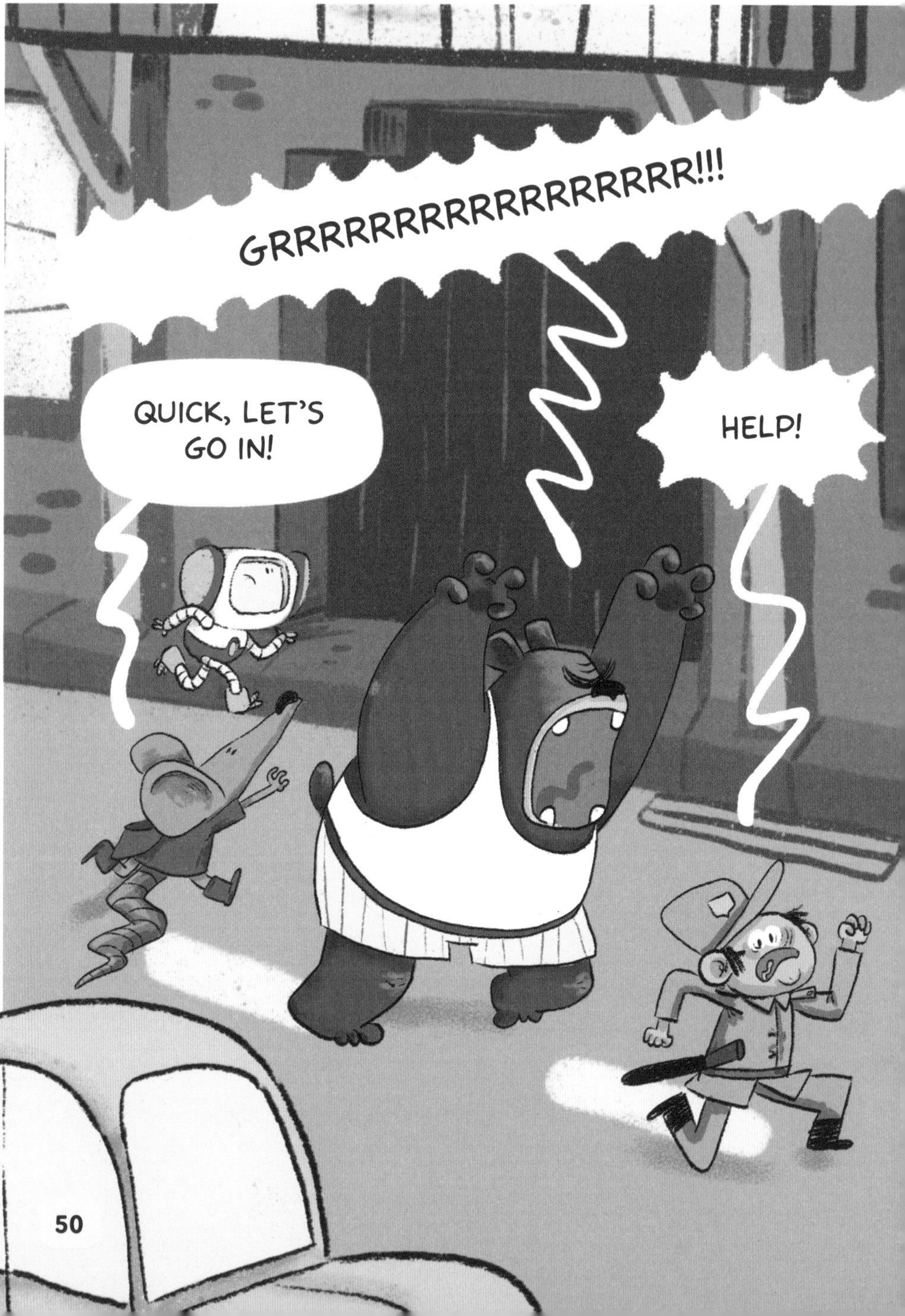
GRRRRRRRRRRRRRRRR!!!
QUICK, LET'S GO IN!
HELP!

WE TRIED TO BE AS QUIET AS POSSIBLE.

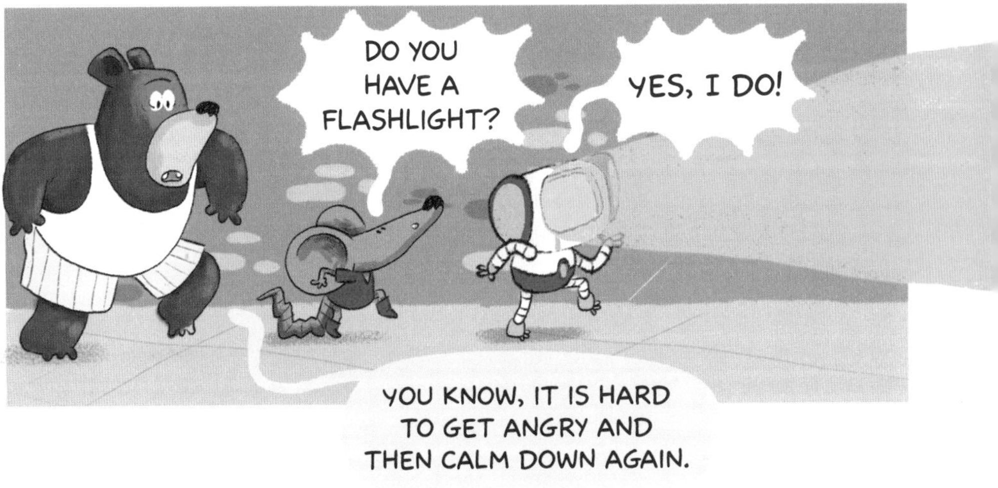
DO YOU HAVE A FLASHLIGHT?
YES, I DO!
YOU KNOW, IT IS HARD TO GET ANGRY AND THEN CALM DOWN AGAIN.

I DISTRACTED WAGNER BY OPENING DOORS.

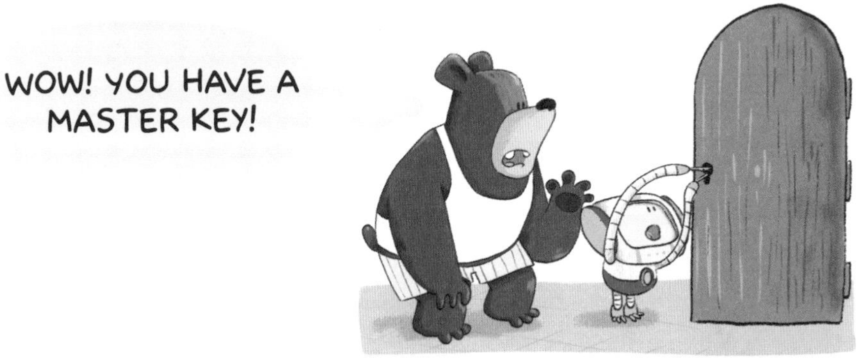
WOW! YOU HAVE A MASTER KEY!

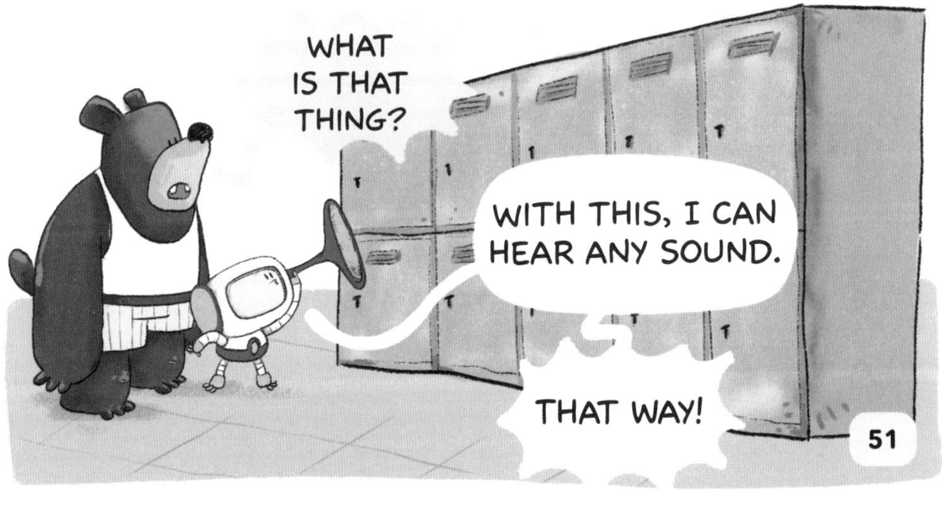
WHAT IS THAT THING?
WITH THIS, I CAN HEAR ANY SOUND.
THAT WAY!

AND THERE HE WAS! WE HAD FOUND HIM.

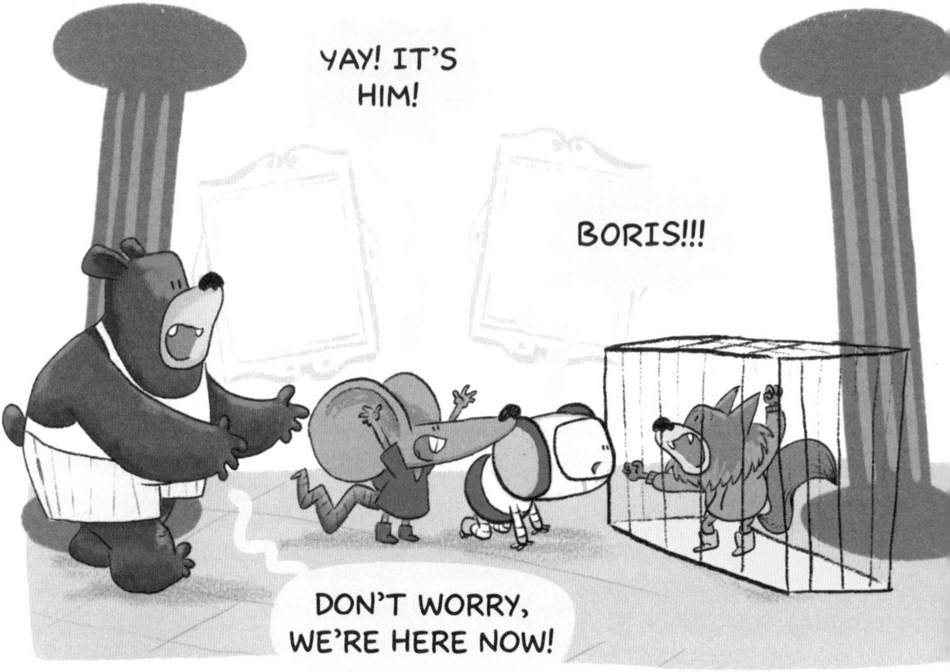
YAY! IT'S HIM!
BORIS!!!
DON'T WORRY, WE'RE HERE NOW!

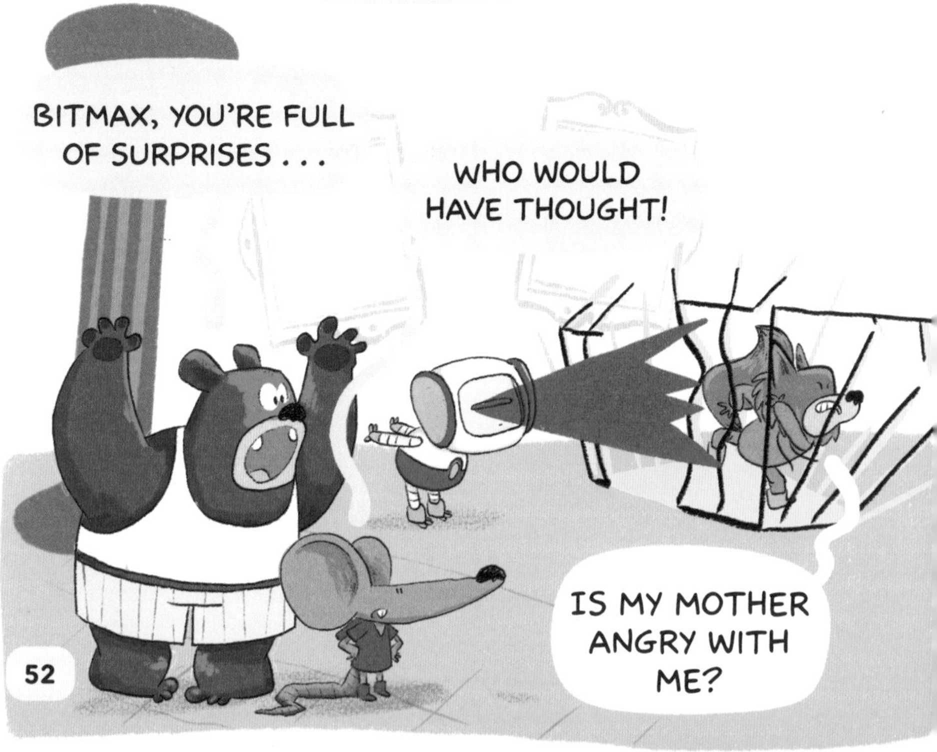
BITMAX, YOU'RE FULL OF SURPRISES . . .
WHO WOULD HAVE THOUGHT!
IS MY MOTHER ANGRY WITH ME?

WE WANTED TO GO BACK TO THE FOREST RIGHT AWAY, BUT IT WASN'T THAT EASY.

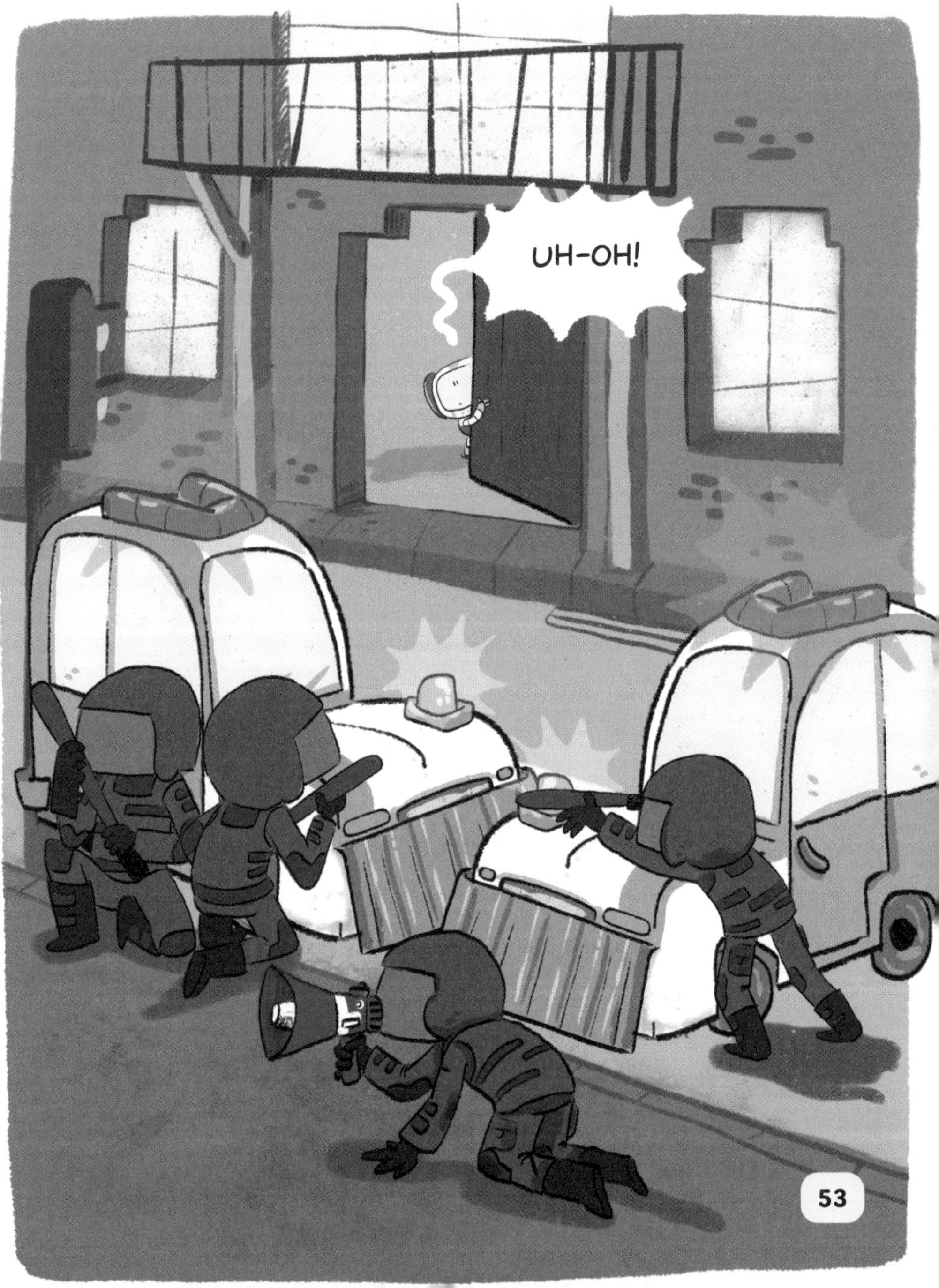
UH-OH!

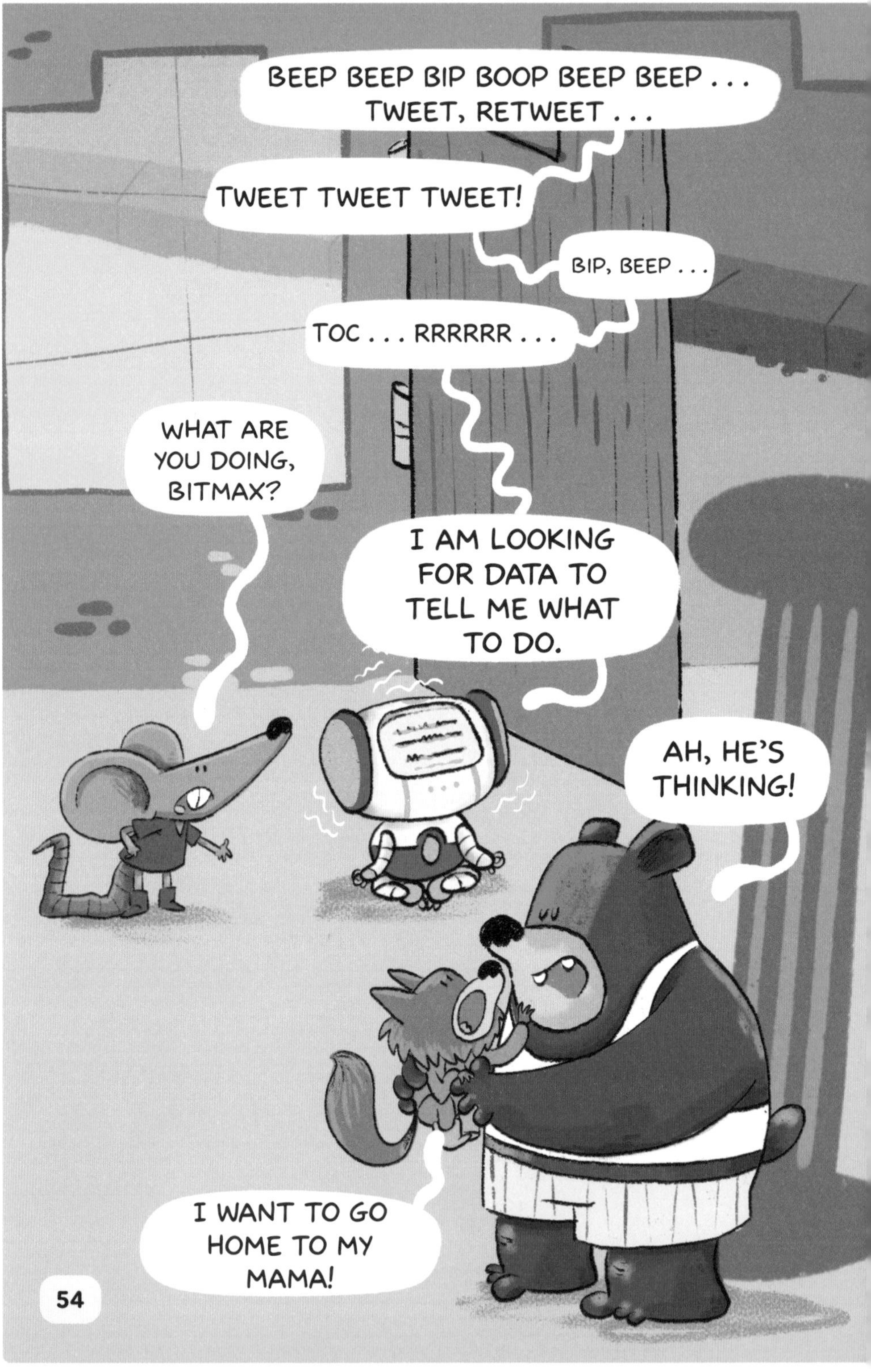
BEEP BEEP BIP BOOP BEEP BEEP . . . TWEET, RETWEET . . .
TWEET TWEET TWEET!
BIP, BEEP . . .
TOC . . . RRRRRR . . .
WHAT ARE YOU DOING, BITMAX?
I AM LOOKING FOR DATA TO TELL ME WHAT TO DO.
AH, HE'S THINKING!
I WANT TO GO HOME TO MY MAMA!

I REMEMBERED THAT WE HAD SEEN SOME LOCKERS. MAYBE THE WORKERS KEPT EXTRA CLOTHES IN THEM.

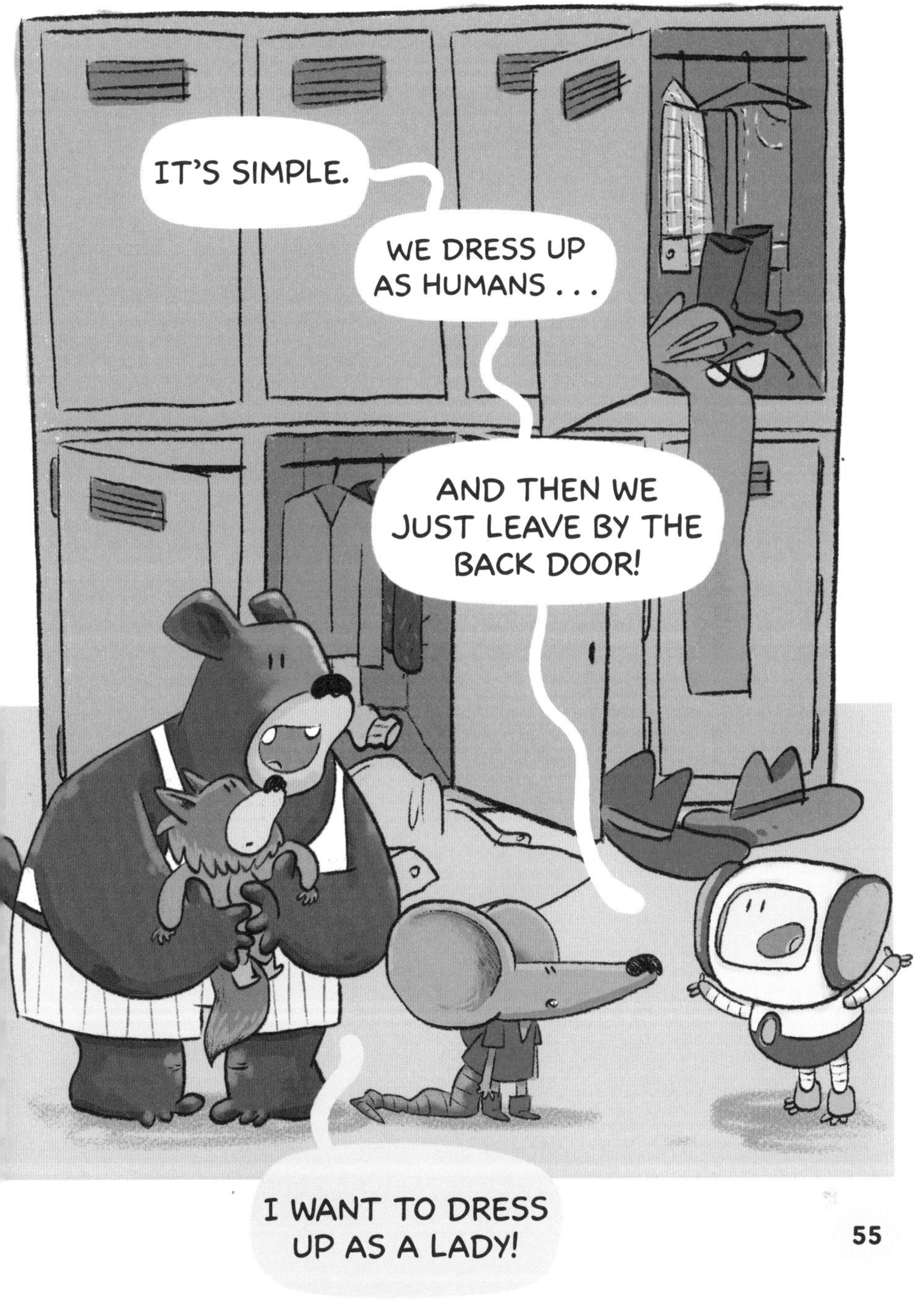
IT'S SIMPLE.
WE DRESS UP AS HUMANS . . .
AND THEN WE JUST LEAVE BY THE BACK DOOR!
I WANT TO DRESS UP AS A LADY!

SO WE DID IT! WE WALKED OUT ONTO THE STREET AND ALMOST PASSED UNNOTICED.

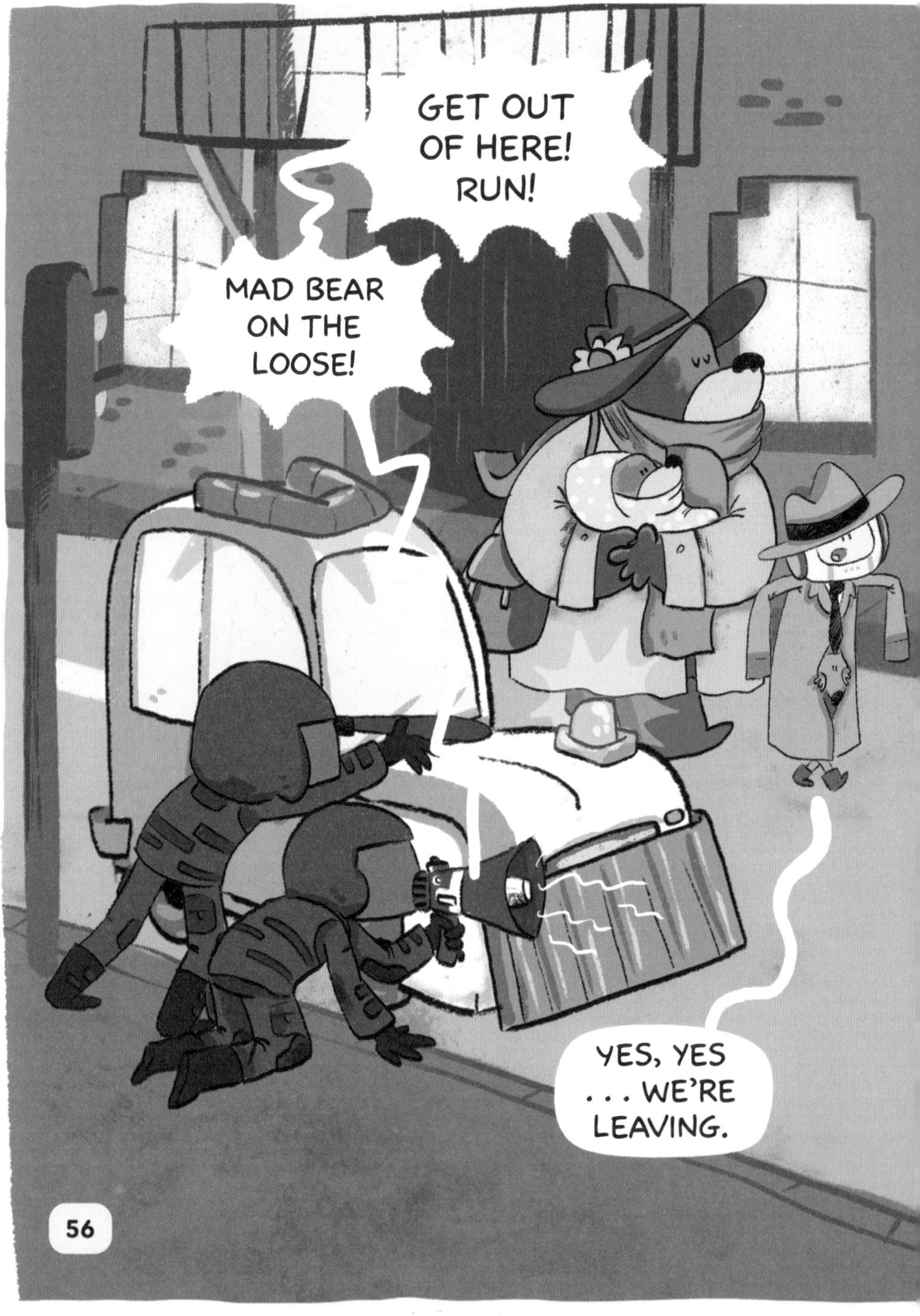
MAD BEAR ON THE LOOSE!
GET OUT OF HERE! RUN!
YES, YES . . . WE'RE LEAVING.

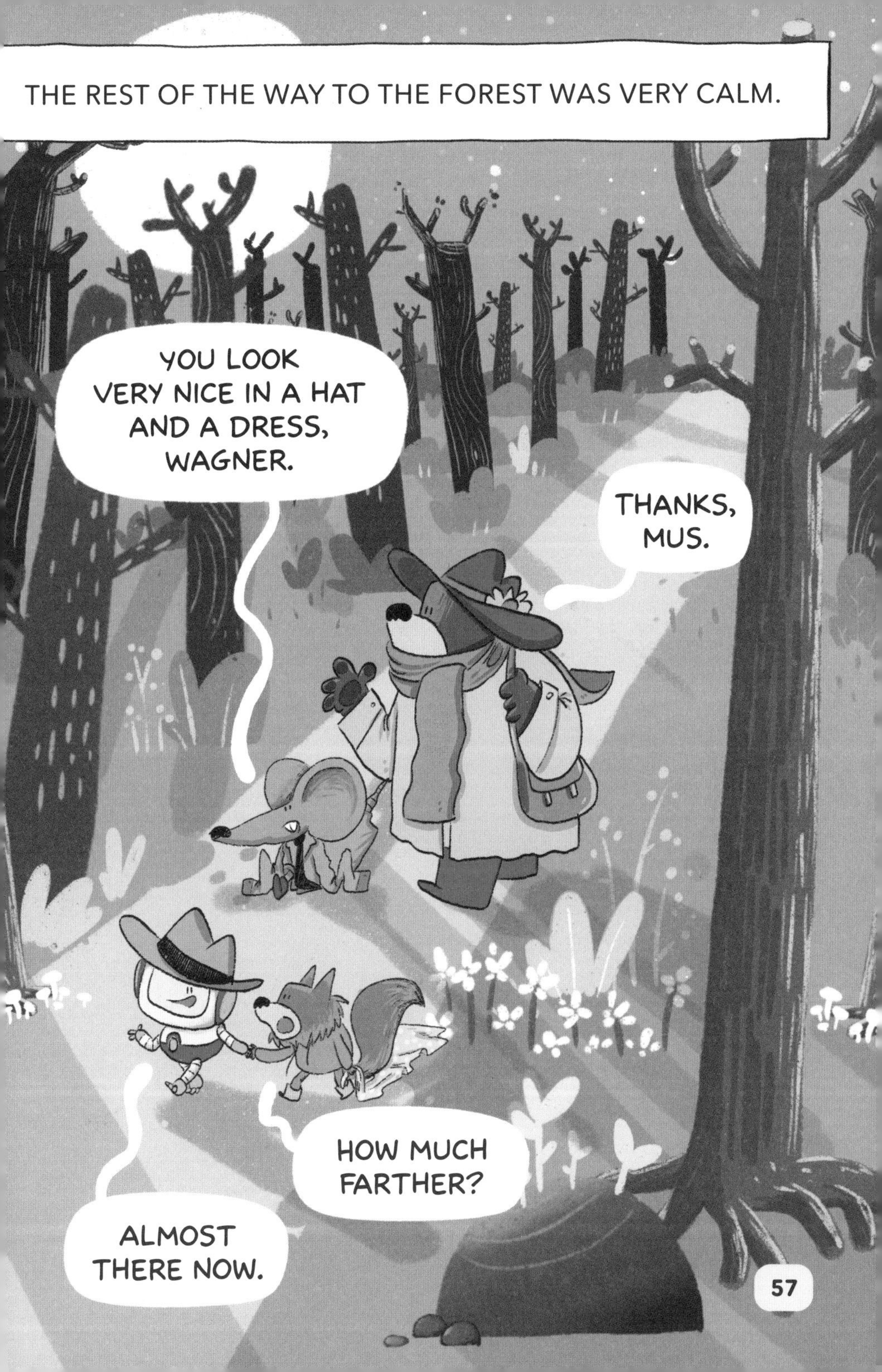
THE REST OF THE WAY TO THE FOREST WAS VERY CALM.
YOU LOOK VERY NICE IN A HAT AND A DRESS, WAGNER.
THANKS, MUS.
HOW MUCH FARTHER?
ALMOST THERE NOW.

PART FIVE

THE
CELEBRATION

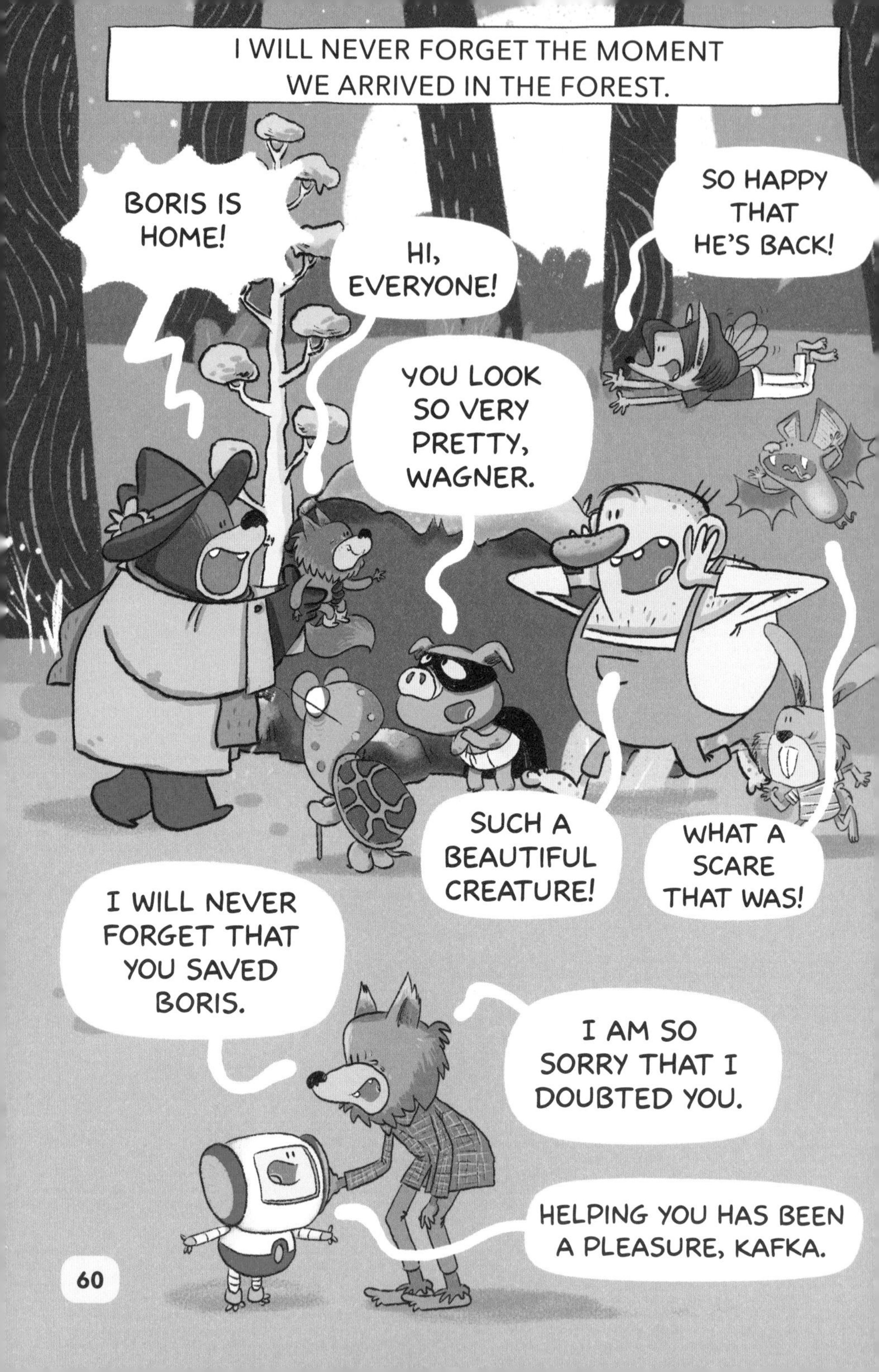
I WILL NEVER FORGET THE MOMENT WE ARRIVED IN THE FOREST.
BORIS IS HOME!
HI, EVERYONE!
SO HAPPY THAT HE'S BACK!
YOU LOOK SO VERY PRETTY, WAGNER.
SUCH A BEAUTIFUL CREATURE!
WHAT A SCARE THAT WAS!
I WILL NEVER FORGET THAT YOU SAVED BORIS.
I AM SO SORRY THAT I DOUBTED YOU.
HELPING YOU HAS BEEN A PLEASURE, KAFKA.

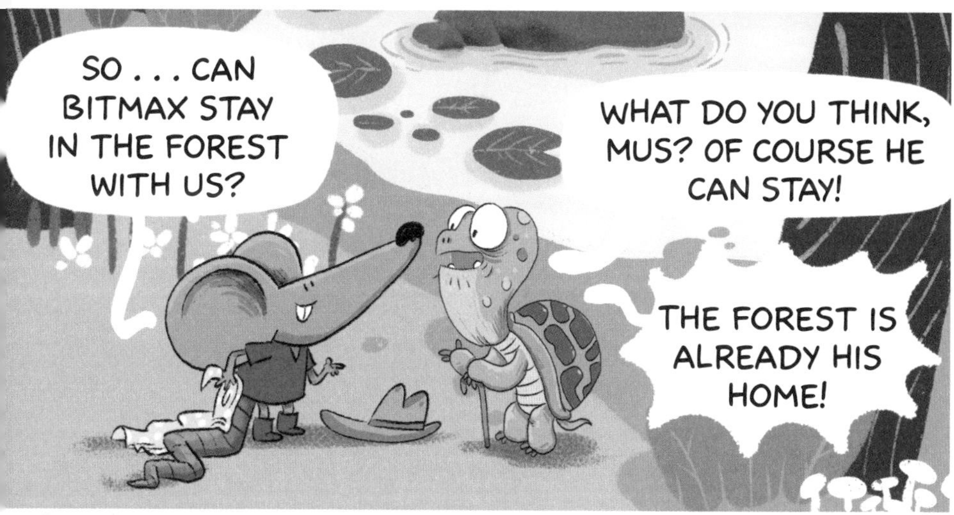
SO . . . CAN BITMAX STAY IN THE FOREST WITH US?
WHAT DO YOU THINK, MUS? OF COURSE HE CAN STAY!
THE FOREST IS ALREADY HIS HOME!

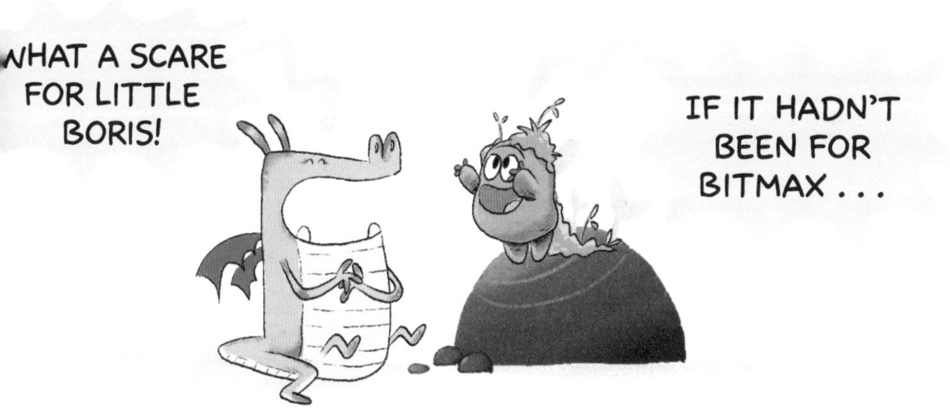
WHAT A SCARE FOR LITTLE BORIS!
IF IT HADN'T BEEN FOR BITMAX . . .

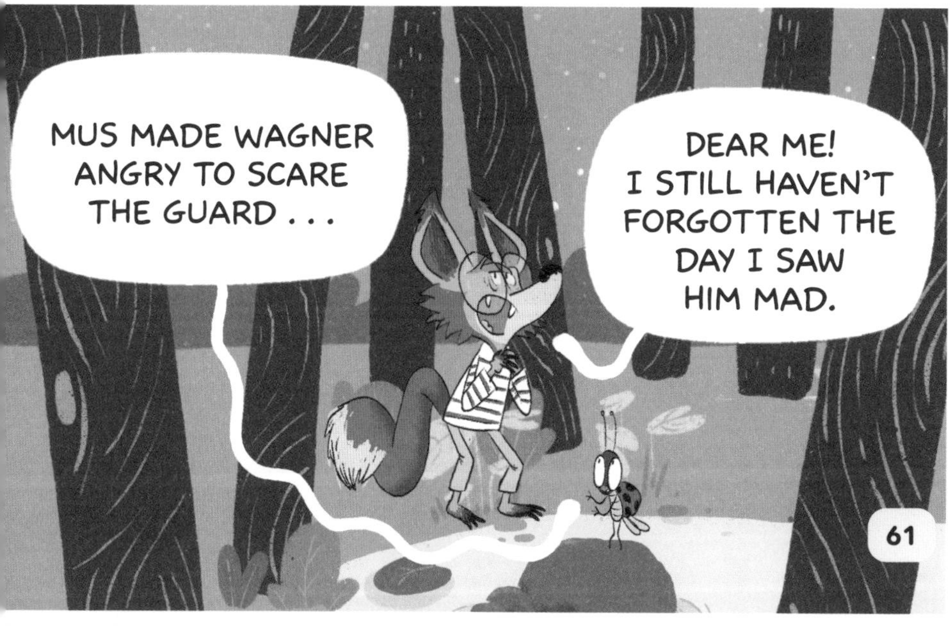
MUS MADE WAGNER ANGRY TO SCARE THE GUARD . . .
DEAR ME! I STILL HAVEN'T FORGOTTEN THE DAY I SAW HIM MAD.

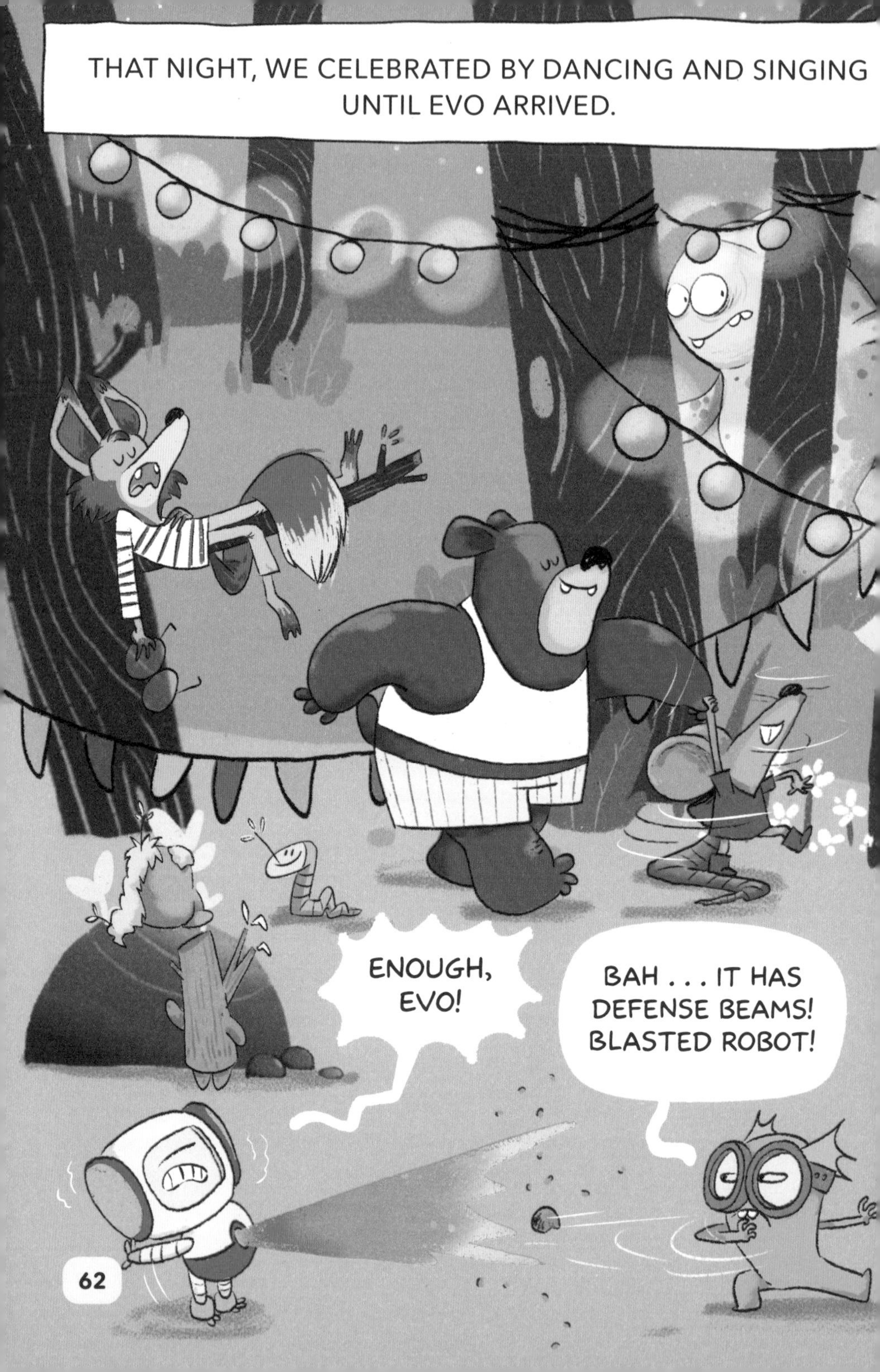
THAT NIGHT, WE CELEBRATED BY DANCING AND SINGING UNTIL EVO ARRIVED.
ENOUGH, EVO!
BAH . . . IT HAS DEFENSE BEAMS! BLASTED ROBOT!

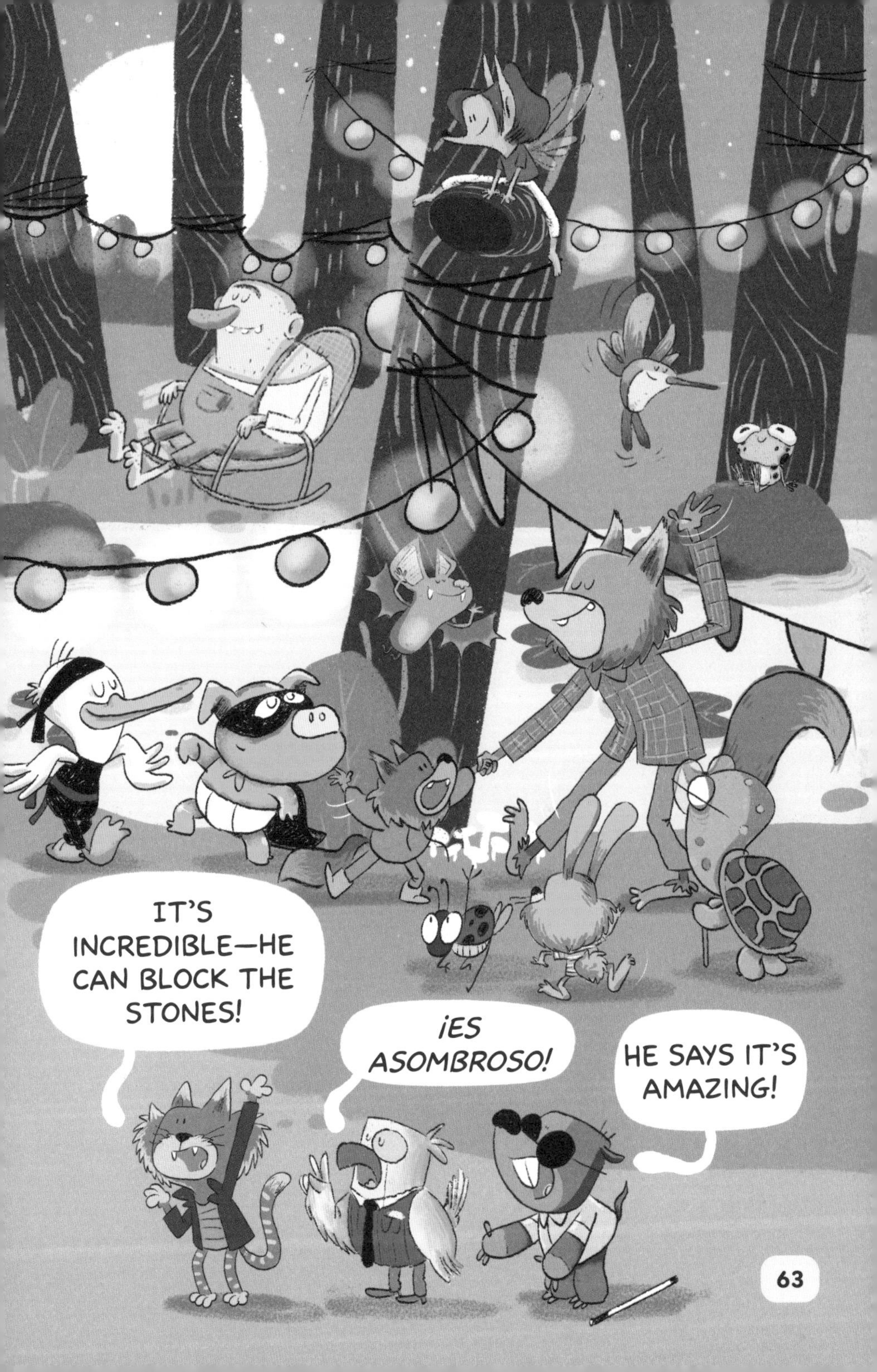
IT'S INCREDIBLE—HE CAN BLOCK THE STONES!
¡ES ASOMBROSO!
HE SAYS IT'S AMAZING!

AS EVO WAS STARTING TO LEAVE, KAFKA LEAPT TOWARD HIM.

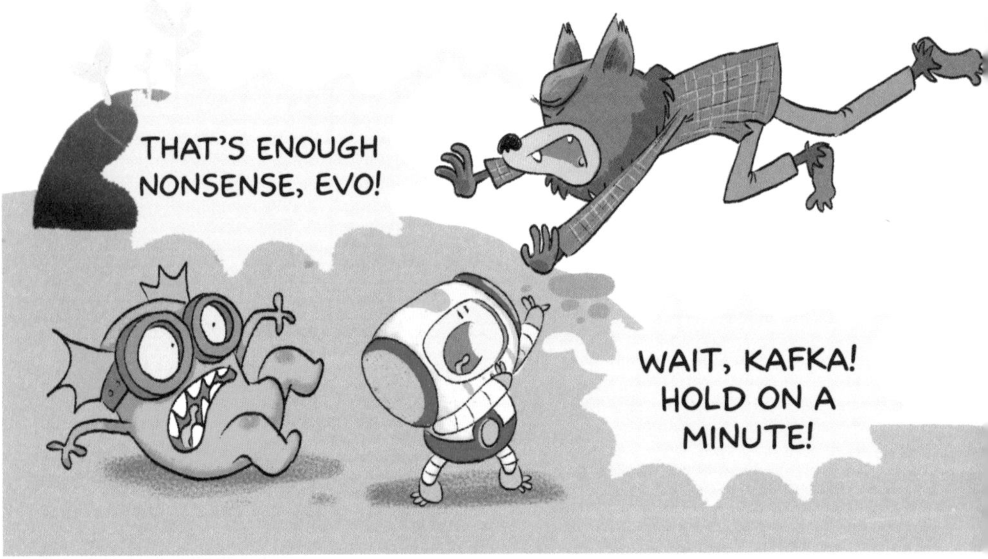
THAT'S ENOUGH NONSENSE, EVO!
WAIT, KAFKA! HOLD ON A MINUTE!

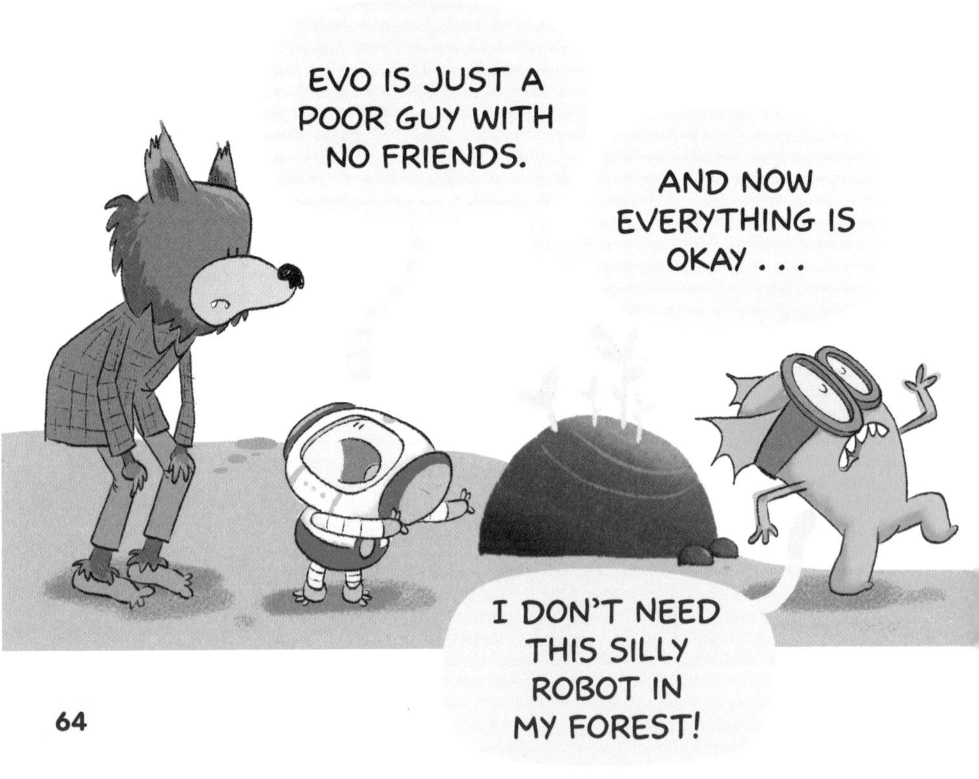
EVO IS JUST A POOR GUY WITH NO FRIENDS.
AND NOW EVERYTHING IS OKAY . . .
I DON'T NEED THIS SILLY ROBOT IN MY FOREST!

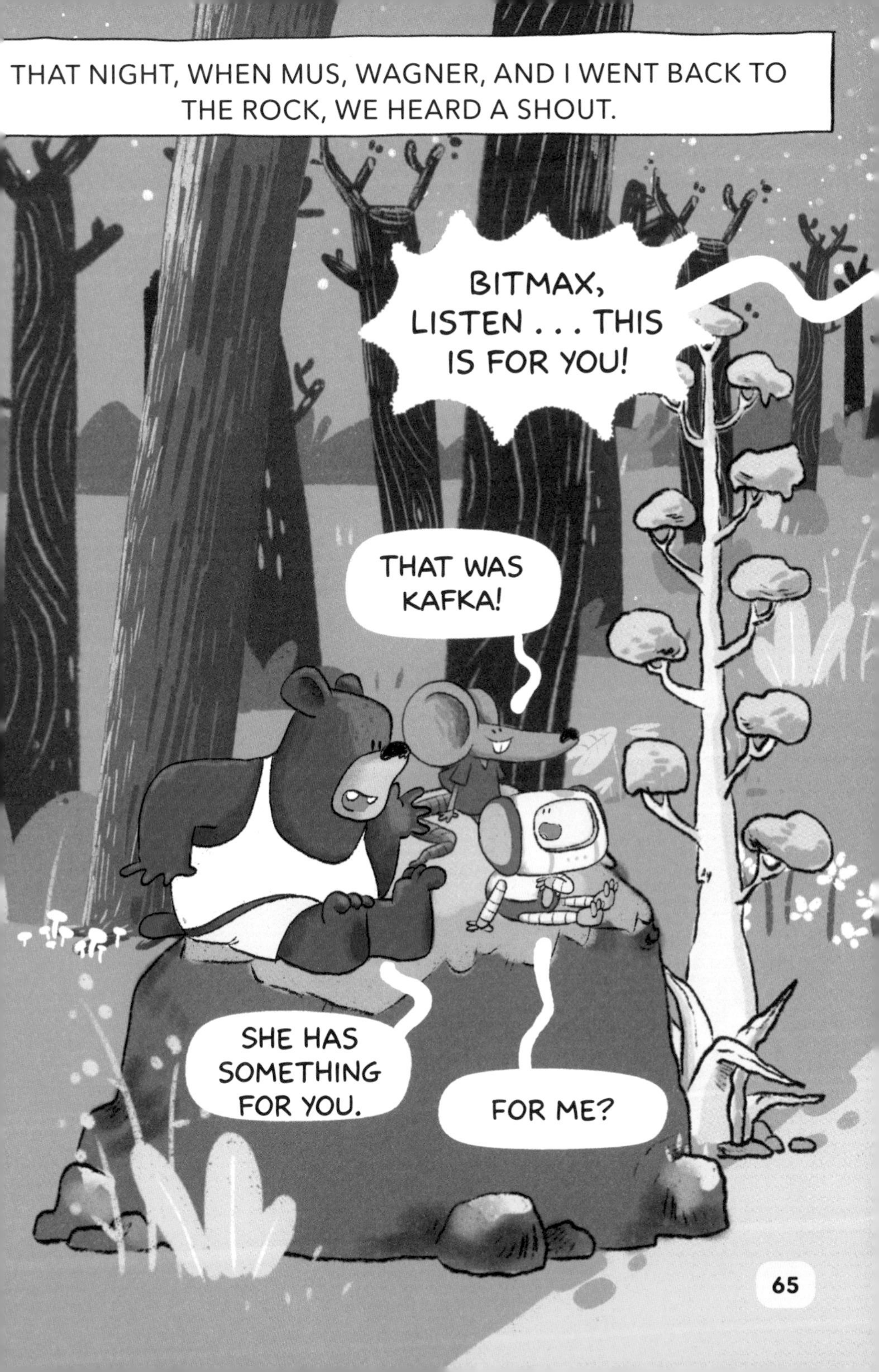
THAT NIGHT, WHEN MUS, WAGNER, AND I WENT BACK TO THE ROCK, WE HEARD A SHOUT.
BITMAX, LISTEN . . . THIS IS FOR YOU!
THAT WAS KAFKA!
SHE HAS SOMETHING FOR YOU.
FOR ME?

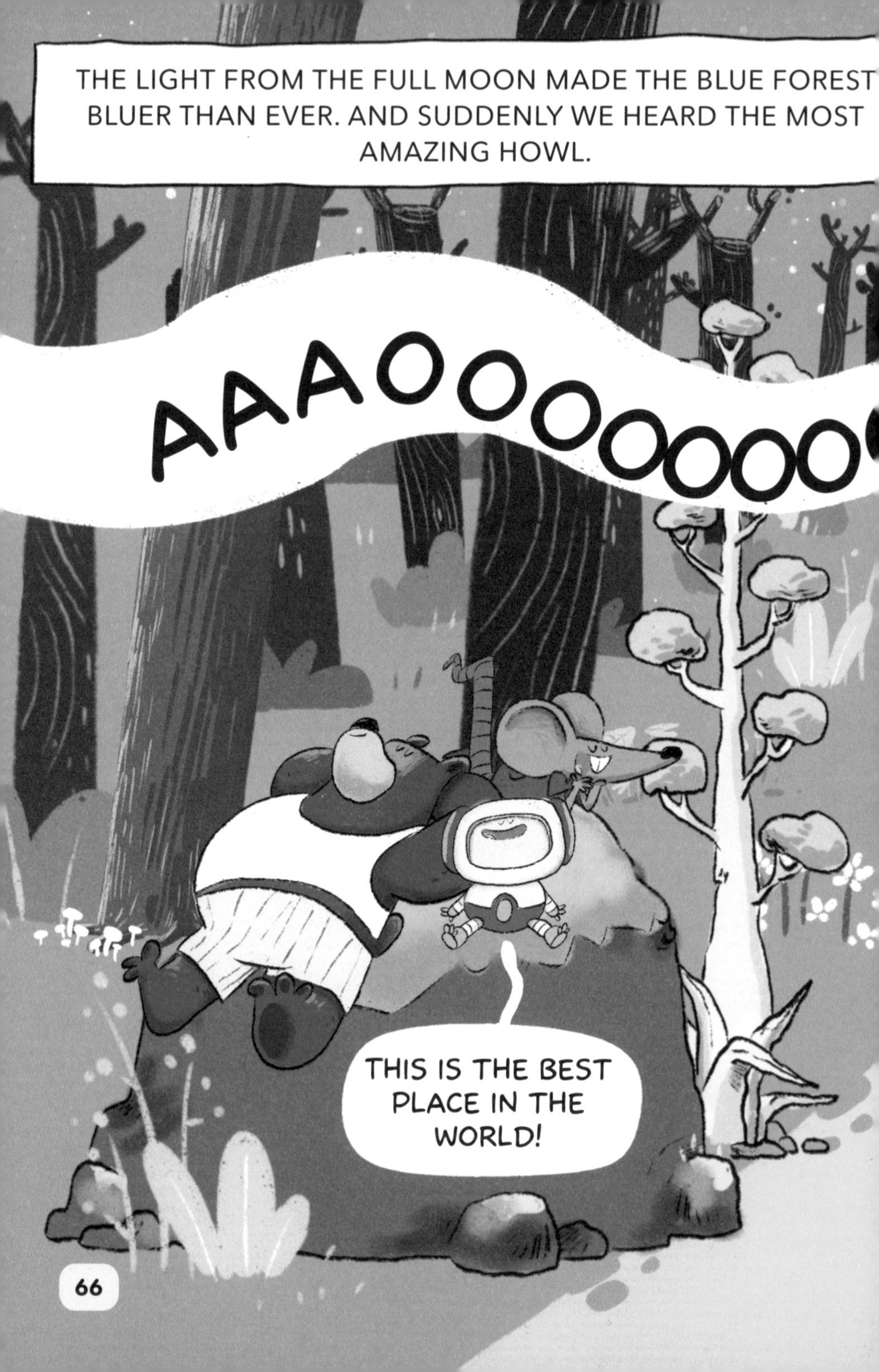
THE LIGHT FROM THE FULL MOON MADE THE BLUE FOREST BLUER THAN EVER. AND SUDDENLY WE HEARD THE MOST AMAZING HOWL.
AAAOOOOOOOO
THIS IS THE BEST PLACE IN THE WORLD!

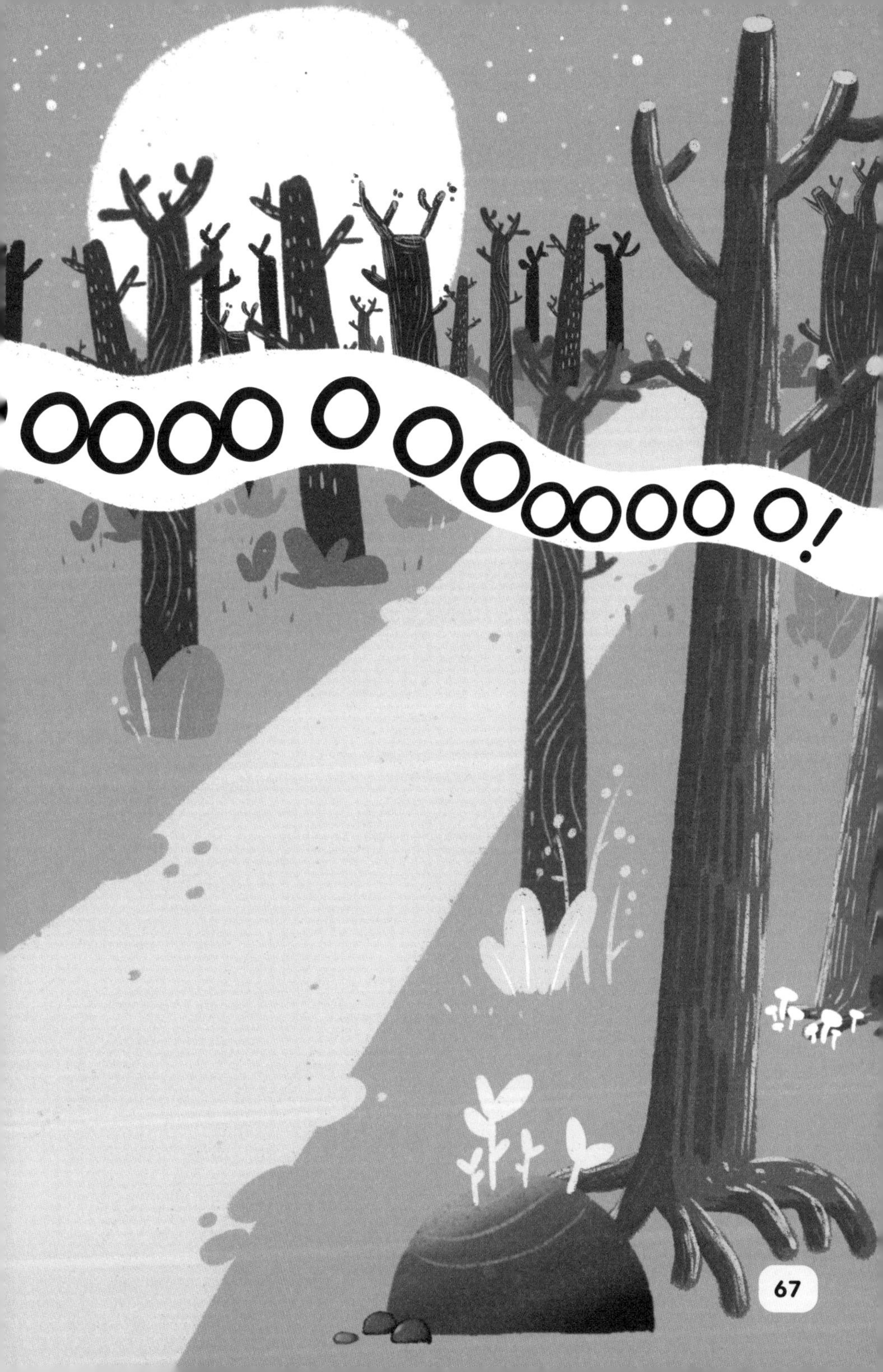
OOOO O OOOOOO O!

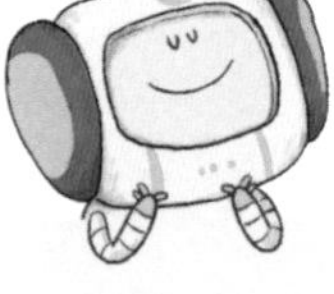

FOLLOW MORE BITMAX & CO. ADVENTURES IN ...

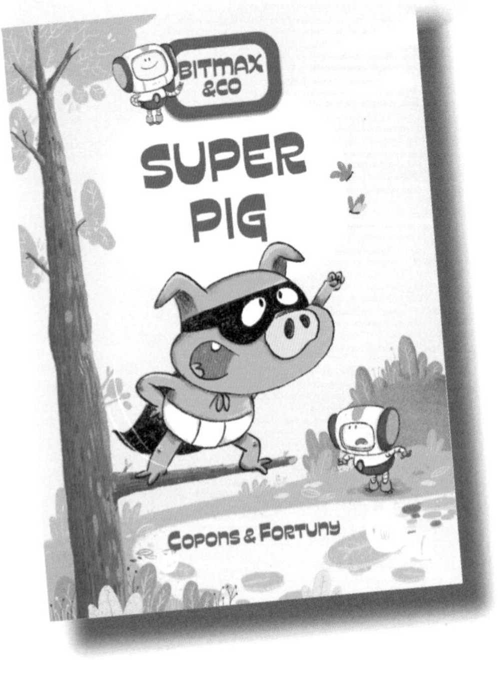
BITMAX &CO
SUPER PIG
Copons & Fortuny

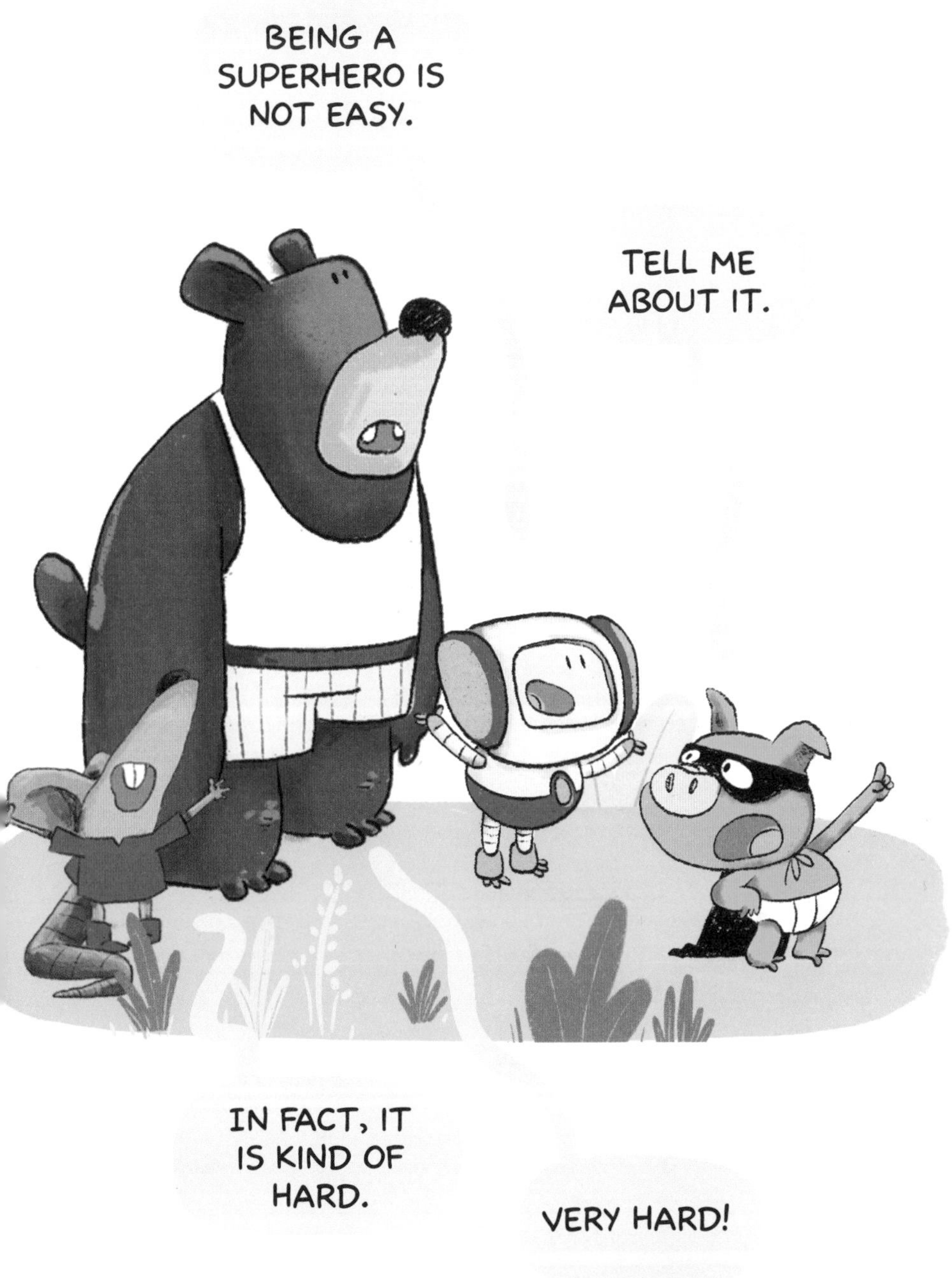
BEING A SUPERHERO IS NOT EASY.
TELL ME ABOUT IT.
IN FACT, IT IS KIND OF HARD.
VERY HARD!

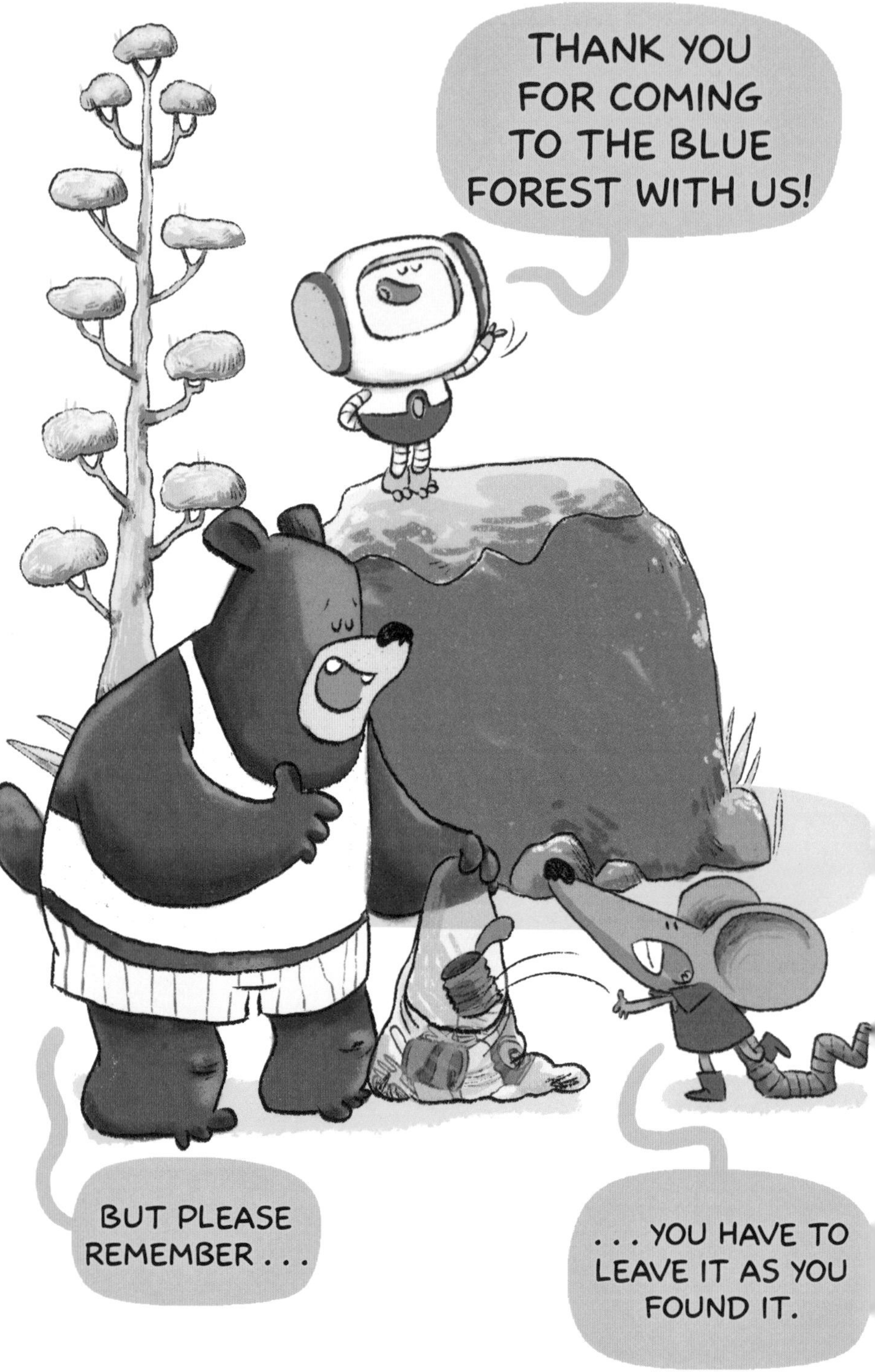
THANK YOU FOR COMING TO THE BLUE FOREST WITH US!
BUT PLEASE REMEMBER . . .
. . . YOU HAVE TO LEAVE IT AS YOU FOUND IT.

WHO IS BEHIND BITMAX & CO.?

THE BITMAX & CO. SERIES OF GRAPHIC NOVELS IS WRITTEN AND DRAWN BY JAUME COPONS AND LILIANA FORTUNY, THE AUTHORS OF THE ALEX AND THE MONSTERS ADVENTURES.

BESIDES HAVING WRITTEN A LOT OF NOVELS, SONGS, AND SCRIPTS, **JAUME COPONS** IS COAUTHOR OF THE *I, ELVIS RIBOLDI* SERIES AND A CREATOR OF TV SERIES FOR CHILDREN. HE LIKES TO WANDER AIMLESSLY, LOOK AT SHOE-STORE WINDOWS, LISTEN TO THE SAME SONG OVER AND OVER, AND READ SEVERAL BOOKS AT THE SAME TIME.

LILIANA FORTUNY DRAWS AND ANIMATES PICTURES. SHE IS COAUTHOR OF *THIS BOOK IS MY GRANDFATHER'S* AND *THIS BOOK IS MY GRANDMOTHER'S*. HALF HER LIFE IS SPENT AMONG ANIMATED FILMS, ALBUM COVER DESIGNS, AND MUSIC VIDEOS. THE OTHER HALF IS ALWAYS INVENTING NEW WORLDS, GOING OUT ONTO THE BALCONY OF HER HOME, EATING ARTICHOKES AND JAPANESE FOOD, AND WATCHING MOVIES.

VISIT US ON THE BITMAX & CO. WEBSITE
SCHIFFER-KIDS.COM/BITMAX